UNFORGETTABLE LOVER

A WARRIORS OF LEMURIA NOVELLA

ROSALIE REDD

UNFORGETTABLE LOVER
A Warriors of Lemuria Novella

By

Rosalie Redd

For permissions contact: Rosalie@rosalieredd.com
Cover Design: Melody Simmons
ISBN: 9781944419035
United States of America

To my father, who always believed in me.

CHAPTER 1

A REMOTE REGION IN THE PACIFIC NORTHWEST

600 YEARS AGO

"**W**hy are we here, Maman?" Leonna raised her hand to shield her eyes from the bright sunlight.

A calm breeze filtered through the pines, whisking through the branches in a soft caress, but the familiar sound didn't calm her nerves. On the contrary, the wind ratcheted up her excitement, her desire, her need. The prospect of participating in the Betram ritual sent a surge of adrenaline into her bloodstream. The evening's rite was her chance to be free, if only for one night.

Maman glanced at her only daughter. Despite the scarf draped over her thin frame, the older female couldn't hide the obvious pain evident in her stiff back. "This is a special place, Lea, one that changed my life. The Rock of Roan can change yours, too."

"You really believe in the power of the stone?" A flutter built in Leonna's gut.

"Roan's rock and the sun brought your father and me together during a Betram ritual." A familiar glimmer crossed her mother's features, and her pale blue eyes held a radiant shine.

A small clearing surrounded the large boulder as if the old growth trees were afraid to get too close. Moss covered the stone's northern edge, and the rock seemed out of place, a relic of a different time.

As Leonna approached the old sentinel, morning dew coated her toes. She glanced at the youth sandals she'd outgrown. New shoes were not an option, not with her father's declining health. She touched the seashell in the center of her necklace. The smooth texture eased the ache in her chest, at least for the moment. With her brother, Corbin, in the tryouts for the warrior class, she was the only one to help her parents with the honey cart. Her sense of honor burned a hole in her soul, but she wouldn't let her parents down.

Maman circled her finger in the air. "Turn around, Lea."

A thrilling shiver crept up Leonna's arms.

Maman's cool fingers caressed the back of her neck as she flipped Leonna's braid over her shoulder. The long hair tickled the skin on her arm leaving a trail of goosebumps in its wake. The chain holding her most precious gift slid from around her neck, and the cherished trinket landed in her palm. The rare shell, gilded in fine gold, reflected the sunlight.

Maman had obtained the rare object in trade from one of the humans who shared the forests and lived in strange dwellings made of mud and wood. Given to her when Leonna was a child, this piece represented hope. Leonna never took the necklace off, even wearing the jewelry to bed. She felt naked without the familiar weight against her chest.

She faced her mother. "What—"

Shhhh. Maman held a finger to her lips. Her eyes sparkled with amusement, the creases of her skin wrinkling, aging her before her time. "You must be ready for the ritual."

The warmth from the early morning sun already coated Leonna's skin in a fine sheen of sweat. The temperature would soar later. Today was the first day of summer, and tonight was the full moon. The occurrence happened approximately every thirty years. The pull of the sun and the moon on the same day brought out their beast, along with the urge to mate.

Betram was a Lemurian festival created to celebrate life and allow the beast the freedom to rut for one night without attachments, without restrictions—and to prevent the havoc that would ensue otherwise. All unbonded males and females of age were required to attend. She'd been a newb during the last ritual, too young to take part in the events. This time, at thirty-two, she was old enough. Now, she couldn't wait to participate.

"What do you need my necklace for?" Her heart tripped at the thought of losing her precious piece.

"The energy from the sun works in tandem with the magic in the stone, infusing the gold with good luck." Maman looked into the distance. A small smile curved her bottom lip. She placed her palm on the rock, caressing the smooth surface with her fingers as if remembering her own ritual many years ago. "Find a place that suits you, and leave the necklace there. Return before nightfall and good luck shall be yours."

Leonna scrunched her eyebrows together. The ritual was all about releasing the beast and letting go, having fun. "But Maman…why do I need luck?"

Maman winked at her. "Many a Stiyaha has found their mate on this night. Perhaps you will as well."

Ugh. Bonding to a male was not something she wanted. She'd already had one relationship that hadn't ended well. She didn't need another one. "Why would I want that? Males are so," she waved her hand in the air, "demanding and possessive."

A thin laugh burst from her mother's throat, startling her. "Yes, but you'll find them alluring and hard to resist tonight."

"That doesn't mean I'm interested in bonding to one of them." Leonna clenched her fist around the shell, the gold chain bouncing against the back of her fingers, teasing them with the promise of hope and love. Her heart skipped a beat, the traitorous organ giving away her innermost desire. She pursed her lips.

"If you don't want to bond, then you won't. The luck is the hope that you will find what you really want, be that love, courage, faith, or whatever your soul craves."

Find what you really want. The words echoed in Leonna's mind. A swell of energy made her chest expand. *I want to paint.* Her love of painting had been instilled in her from an early age. She still remembered her first brush and how she'd swayed to her own rhythm, creating her painted canvases. Others had marveled at her work, commending her for her style and attention to detail.

A sharp pain radiated from her chest. That was before the accident.

Leonna looked at her index finger, the one remaining digit on her right hand. She still painted, when she could get away from her responsibilities at the family honey cart. The paintings were good, but she'd lost her special touch. With a loud exhale, she bit her lip.

Maman placed a warm hand on her forearm. "My daughter, fear not. My maman did this for me at my first Betram ritual, as her maman did for her. This necklace," she touched Leonna's closed fist, "was made for this very occasion. I gave the shell to you on your first birthday in anticipation of tonight."

Leonna stared into her maman's eyes, moist with unshed tears. Her chest tightened at the realization of how much her maman loved her. She threw her arms around her mother's neck. The scent of cherries filled Leonna's senses, and her heart swelled all the more.

"Thank you, Maman," she whispered.

Stepping back, she studied the boulder, searching for the perfect spot. Placing the gilded shell on a small bump, she gently straightened the chain, making sure as much gold as possible absorbed the sun's rays. She'd be back before nightfall to collect the precious gift. A lump formed in her throat. Now, if she only knew what she really wanted.

CHAPTER 2

*N*icholai buttoned his pants and tightened the belt around his waist. The bare skin on his chest and arms crawled with his frustration. A sharp pulse on his shoulder caught his attention. He touched his marking for duty, the innermost circle of three. The dark line burned, a message that he would do what was expected of him. As a result, the second ring also heated as his conviction took hold. Last, but not least, his outer marking, the one for courage raged to life. He'd need all three values to get through the night.

He grabbed his button-down shirt from the back of his desk chair and threw it on. The material, made of fine cotton caressed his skin, but did nothing to calm his anxiety. A loud exhale whooshed from his lips.

He sat down on the carved wooden chair. The lumber creaked in protest, the familiar sound giving him some reprieve. Tonight was Betram, and wasn't that grand. He clenched his teeth. As with all the unbonded males, he had to participate. Whether he wanted to or not was of no concern, and he cared not.

He gripped the edge of his boot and shoved his foot into the worn leather. The laces groaned their complaint as he cinched them tight. He put on the other shoe and repeated the process. Standing, he glanced at his sword leaning against the wall. As if sensing his interest, the blade tittered, eager for a night on the battlefield.

"Not tonight, my friend." He shook his head and patted the dagger attached to his belt. This was his only protection this evening if he encountered any Gossum. The evil creatures were his kind's bitter enemy in the game the gods played in their bid for Earth. Even though he was prince, and expected someday to become king of the Stiyaha, he was just another piece in their game.

He didn't like thinking about the never-ending war. The gods and their battles were the reason they were on this planet—to fight for Earth and its precious water. If his side won, the Lemurians would trade knowledge with the humans for access to water. If they lost, the Gossum would enslave humankind, taking the water by force.

The Gossum were a constant threat.

He was ready, but his feet remained in place. Wiping his hand over his face, he exhaled. Most males looked forward to Betram when their beast could roam free, enjoying the chance to frolic and play, but most of all, to rut with the females without any obligations. Although he longed to be like the other males, eager to partake, he dreaded the ritual.

There was always the chance that his beast would bond him to a female. He'd had a few relationships along the way, mainly physical. Once the female started to get too close, emotionally, he'd end the affair. As a result, he'd earned the reputation of a heartbreaker. Can't say he didn't deserve it.

If he could control his beast tonight, he'd take the less used option to stay in human form. He'd have to hunt a female that does the same.

Knock. Knock.

He jumped at the sound. Sunstones lining the Keep's walls brightened, the warmth intended to sooth his jittery nerves. The underground Keep watched out for him, tending to his need for shelter and warmth as best she could. "Enter."

The old oak door swung open on its hinge without a sound. A cool breeze filtered in through the doorway, along with the scent of tarragon.

Thump. Thump. Gaetan, the Keep's *Haelen*, their healer, and the closest friend Nicholai had, walked into the room. His cane tapped against the stone floor in a steady rhythm. His deformed leg made him lean to the left. Although he could walk without the staff, he preferred the cane for support.

Nicholai refused to get close to any of the warriors. Making friends meant caring about someone else, and he wouldn't risk their lives, not after losing Rand. His chest tightened at the painful memory. Gaetan couldn't fight with his bad leg, so he never left the Keep to battle the enemy. That made him safe to befriend. Their camaraderie had grown over the years, and Nicholai didn't know what he would do if he was responsible for any injury to his companion.

Gaetan studied him, his gaze roaming Nicholai's outfit. "You ready?"

"I suppose." Nicholai pursed his lips.

A slow smile crept across Gaetan's face. He pointed at Nicholai's hand. "You planning on wearing that?"

Nicholai peered at his finger. As he moved his hand, the sunstone ring reflected the light. His father had given him the jewelry as a birthday present a few years ago when he'd transitioned from a mid-youth to a young male. The jewelry would announce to all participants he was the prince, and that wouldn't do.

"Good point." He removed the ring and placed it in the cup on his dresser next to his razor and his brush, all lined up just like he liked them. He gripped his shoulder, where his marking lay beneath the material. He'd have to remember to keep his shirt on or he'd be recognized. As he glanced at his ring, an empty spot formed in his chest—he hadn't realized how much his father's gift had meant to him.

This reminded him he needed to find an appropriate gift for his father's upcoming one-thousandth birthday. To reach the age of mid-life was a milestone among the Stiyaha. Since his father was king, the responsibility for finding the best gift rested on Nicholai's and his brother's shoulders. *What will Tiernan get him? Eh, it matters not.* For as long as Nicholai could remember, his younger brother had challenged him at every opportunity. The constant bickering and backbiting had driven an irreparable wedge between them.

He took a gander at Gaetan. "Any suggestions on a gift for my father? I'm open to ideas."

The end of Gaetan's staff connected with the stone floor with a loud crack. He chuckled. "No way. Not going there. That's your burden to carry."

"You are ever so helpful." Nicholai raised his eyebrow, but he couldn't help the smirk that pulled at his lip. "I don't know which is worse, searching for a present for my finicky father or going to Betram."

"Present searching. Hands down." Gaetan leaned against the back of Nicholai's chair. "Betram is supposed to be fun. Why you can't see it that way, I'll never understand."

Nicholai tensed. His gaze caught Gaetan's. "Each to their own. I do this because it's required of all unbonded males."

Gaetan shrugged. "Are you letting the beast out or do you have a mask?"

The creature woke inside him. The synapses in his brain linked them together, and he understood clearly what it wanted—to bond to a female. Deep inside, his inner beast longed for a mate and the young that would come from the bonding. A surge of blood pooled in his groin at the thought. He clenched his jaw. Although he and his beast were one, the human side had the advantage of rational thought. That's why the Stiyaha only transformed during battles and the Betram ritual.

Before answering his friend, he strode over to his bed and picked up the mask that lay on the covers. He held it up. "Got what I need, right here."

His gaze roamed Gaetan. He wore his usual loose fitting pants, the ones that concealed his weakness. His brown woven top had a flared collar and short sleeves. His marking ran down his right arm and ended in four fine lines on his hand. He didn't have a mask.

"I take it your beast is leading the way tonight." Nicholai nodded.

"As the Keep's Haelen, I don't get the opportunity to get out much. So, yes."

"Well then, let's get this over with." Nicholai placed the mask over his head. The tight skin covered his hair. Holes cut in the material for his eyes hid his eyebrows. The black-dyed leather ended in a long point over the bridge of his nose. The mask was standard issue for all participants. *The veil better work.*

CHAPTER 3

*T*he summer solstice sun hung on the edge of the horizon. The last of the warm rays colored the scattered clouds a vibrant pink. Leonna's heart picked up its pace. A case of the giggles bubbled up, and she clamped her hand over her mouth to keep them inside.

Dozens of females stood at the edge of the forest, and more emerged from the portal. Through the opening, Rin, one of the Keep's Jixies, stood over the *porte stanen*. His hands moved to a rhythm all his own, his fingers coaxing the mist to rise and swirl. A female wearing a short skirt and a tight-fitting blouse emerged through the haze and landed a few feet away. Her style of clothing, with its sequined jewels, gave away her status as one of the elite, most likely a council member's daughter. There was no way to know for sure, the mask covering her face was similar to the one Leonna wore, as did all the females.

The dampness of the condensation caused by the portal coated Leonna's arms. A shiver ran over her shoulders, whether from the coolness or her own excitement, she wasn't quite sure.

"Honey, come. Let's head over to the fire before the crowd gets too thick." Chantel pulled on Leonna's arm.

Leonna turned to her best friend and couldn't contain the squeal any longer. She grabbed her companion's hands, and they both shook from their combined excitement. "I've waited for this night for a long time. I can't believe it's finally here."

"Yes, I know. You've been talking non-stop about Betram for months." Chantel rolled her eyes. Despite the dark cloth that covered the top of her head and part of her face, her expression of utter disdain was clearly visible in the darkening light.

"Have you decided yet? Are you going to remove your mask?" Leonna followed her friend toward the crowd forming around the large bonfire.

"Yes. I'm going beast. Why not? That's what we're here for, right?"

Chantel's tight dress fit snug over her ample bosom and show-cased her long, supple legs. Blond hair the color of straw cascaded over her shoulders, and her soft, plump lips were an enticement all their own. A pang of doubt weighed on Leonna's chest. Her own body was lean, more muscle and fewer curves than that of her friend. Would a male be interested in her?

She bit her lip. Then, there was her hand. She held up her glove for inspection. Could anyone tell that the last three fingers on her right hand weren't real? That they were just bits of stuffed material? No way would she remove them tonight and expose herself, so letting her beast free was not an option.

In beast form, they would know each other, but because of the fevered intensity of the Betram ritual, the beasts would forget soon after the mating. Fleeting memories of scent, taste, or sound would be all that remained. However, anyone out there could recognize her misshapen hand. She exhaled and closed her eyes.

She wouldn't begrudge her best friend's happiness. After all, she'd promised herself a good time and nothing more. This was her chance to be free, let the feeling and emotions of the ritual take her, like a leaf on the surface of a stream.

Tomorrow, she had to get back to her *responsibilities*. If only she could plan her own life, make her own decisions about what she wanted to do, but no. She'd go back to the honey cart, day after day, and help her parents as expected.

The way her father's health had deteriorated over the past few months, she'd been lucky to find any time to paint. A raw ache radiated from her chest. She couldn't imagine losing him.

She shook her head and held up her chin. No matter what happened, she'd enjoy tonight. The good news—as a species, the Stiyaha didn't need to worry about contracting sexually transmitted diseases. The natural immunity within their Lemurian blood kept any nasty microbes away.

"Gather 'round! Gather 'round!" The loud female voice pulled Leonna from her reverie.

A tall female Stiyaha stood close to the bonfire. She didn't wear a mask. Two black marks marred her left cheek, the sign of a bonded female. Leonna recognized Trian. Her mate's personal mark was two lines that ran down his right cheek. Once bonded the females took the opposite of their mate's marking. Trian and Eliah had a good relationship revealed by the two black bands circling Eliah's throat. During the physical bonding process, the number of black bands was always a mystery until they formed. For those unlucky couples who only received one band, the chances of having a happy life together did not bode well.

"Unbonded females, welcome to Betram. I am Trian." The large female scanned the crowd, as if ensuring she had everyone's attention.

The crowd calmed. Conversations quieted.

The smell of pine mixed with the scents of the females. Each possessed a unique fragrance, which was good since some females had a brother participating in the rite. They would recognize the scent and avoid each other.

"It has been thirty years since the last Betram. You are lucky to participate, not everyone gets that chance. Some end up bonded before the next ritual comes around." Trian touched her cheek.

"Females in the beginning stages of heat—if any of you sense the change coming upon you, please return to the Keep before Rin closes the portal. The last time a female went into heat during Betram, it caused a fight." Trian scanned the faces in the crowd, and her green eyes cast an eerie glow as if lit from within. "Several males died in the process."

The risk of pregnancy during Betram was something to avoid. Pregnant, unbonded females were frowned upon in their society. Leonna was glad she'd never had the urge come upon her, not yet anyway.

"I...I should go back." The female in the short skirt and tight blouse Leonna had seen earlier spoke up from the back of the crowd. "I have a dull ache near my..." She blushed and looked at the ground.

"Thank you for your honesty." Trian nodded at the female.

The young Stiyaha dragged her feet through the grass, heading toward the portal.

"Anyone else?"

When there was no further response, Trian waved a hand at Rin to close the portal. The opening in the mist contracted until the haze disappeared altogether. Darkness crept up from the trees, the last rays of the setting sun now hidden behind the giant mountain.

"The males are stationed in a location several miles away. Their beasts will rule, seeking out the opportunity to mate. They will search for you, hunt you down. Enjoy yourselves." Trian's mouth twisted into a mischievous smile.

Leonna's heart pounded, excitement sending a tingle along her nerves.

"Once you feel the daylight let go, you are free to run, to let the beast rule. Remember, be back in the Keep before dawn. If you encounter any Gossum, slay them...or run." Trian raised her chin, her dark hair falling around her shoulders. "Good luck, may you find what you seek."

Leonna touched the gilded shell that rested between the "V" of her breasts. She'd left it in the sun all day, infusing the jewelry with energy and, hopefully, luck. Her chest tightened, and she frowned. She wasn't sure what she really wanted anymore. That scared her more than anything.

The glow from the sun disappeared. The full moon took its

rightful place in the sky. Deep inside, Leonna's beast recognized the sign. A small growl burst from her throat, and she ran.

CHAPTER 4

*N*icholai's heart thumped against his chest, sending adrenaline through his body, stoking his need—his desire to mate. The combination of the summer sun and the full moon stirred his beast. Their normal symbiotic relationship was never as tight as it was now. Nicholai ran through the forest. The dew from the evening's mist coated the leaves, slapping against his face, his arms, his pants.

Aayieeee. Another male up ahead let loose an exuberant cry. A female must be near.

Nicholai stopped next to a large pine tree to assess his surroundings. The pointed branches reminded him of his enemy's sharp claws. If he ran across a Gossum tonight, his adversary better run. An encounter with the Gossum was part of the thrill of Betram—an added risk, requiring added precaution.

Before the ritual had been integrated into the Earth colony inhabitants, numerous deaths had occurred inside the underground Keep on a night such as this. Beasts ran free, uncontrolled by their human side. The devastation had been significant. Many lives were lost.

Betram became the outlet, the release their beasts desperately needed on this night when the sun and the moon pulled them apart yet pushed them together. The pressure was enough to drive the beast to near insanity. Without help and guidance from the logical human side, bedlam would prevail.

He inhaled, taking a large breath of cool, fresh air into his lungs. A myriad of scents registered in his mind—wet ferns, pine, deer, and the sweet fragrance of female Stiyahas. The concoction blended into a potpourri of aromas, but one stood out from the rest—sweet honey. That particular female called to him. A need like he'd never felt before well up inside, and the surge of adrenaline he'd been riding sprinted through his blood. He couldn't stop himself if he'd tried.

Aayieeee. He let out a cry, half animal, half human. Farther into the forest he ran, tracking the female. His desire to find *her*, the female with the honeyed scent drove him forward. Every time he got close, she eluded him.

An unlucky Douglas fir took a beating as he unleashed his pent up aggression on the poor tree's branches. The last thing he wanted was to injure the female during their coupling. The physical exertion helped ease the ache in his chest.

He stopped to catch his breath. As the night air rushed in and out of his lungs, other females' scents called to him, but the allure of the honeyed female had him hooked. She toyed with him, leading him on, playing her game. He'd find her, of that, he had no doubt.

A surge of heat raced over his arms and back. The woven shirt stuck to his ribs like a second skin. He couldn't take the sweaty cloth anymore and, without thought, ripped the offending material from his body. Buttons flew through the air. A nearby fern cushioned the damaged shirt's fall.

He quieted. His beast took in the sights and sounds around him.

Grunt. Groan. Thump, thump, thump.

A mating nearby sent blood rushing to his groin. The top of the male's head bobbed to their rhythm. In his beast form, wisps of his brown fur moved in the breeze like tall blades of grass. Beady eyes projected from beneath a heavy brow, and pointed tusks protruded from his mouth.

Nicholai averted his gaze. He wanted nothing to do with the

couple in the bushes, but his body responded, his pants painfully tight from his erection. Adjusting himself, he concentrated on tracking his female.

Hour after hour she led him on the chase, but he refused to give up, to search out another. She was his prize and he wouldn't stop. The full moon taunted him, as if laughing at his progress, or lack thereof. He clenched his teeth. Down by the river, he paused by a boulder to catch his breath.

Her unique scent became stronger.

She was close by.

He almost surrendered to the urge to shift into his beast, but he held fast. Larger than most of the Stiyaha, he didn't want to hurt her in his beast form. Besides, he wanted to minimize the risk of a bonding and staying in human form increased his odds.

Movement behind a tree caught his eye. His pinpoint vision picked up a wisp of blond hair turned silvery in the moonlight. The delicate locks appeared soft like the tufts of milkweed seeds. The tips of his fingers tingled as if eager to touch the silken strands.

His beast roared inside, but he didn't make a sound, not wanting to give himself away. He tracked her, the scent of honey filtering into his soul, burning her brand on him. As he got closer, his need to rut caused his shaft to harden in his pants. The strain made him edgy, eager.

She must've sensed him, for she bolted, leaving the safety of her hiding spot behind an old oak.

The chase was on, but they weren't alone.

Another male burst from behind a giant fir, hot on her trail. Determination burned in Nicholai's gut—he wouldn't let the other male win. He focused on the competition, taking him down with a swift tackle. In beast form, the other male was stronger, but Nicholai used his quick hands to bash the male's ears. The beast let out a howl and scrambled away, into the forest.

As his opponent retreated, the surrounding quiet enveloped Nicholai. He searched for the female among the trees. Her scent indicated she was still near. He crept between the giant firs, eager for another glimpse. Not far away, she sprinted from behind a large boulder.

As they raced through the trees, Nicholai caught glimpses of her fine figure. A dark short sleeved shirt fitted her body, accentuating her firm breasts. Long, elegant legs couldn't hide beneath the short skirt that accentuated her hips. Black gloves covered her hands, extending mid-way up her forearms. Each time he spotted her, he learned more about the female he pursued. She intrigued him, and he intensified the hunt.

He closed the distance in a matter of moments. The excitement of the chase and the thrill of the catch were like a drug in his system. He craved more.

As he took her down, he expected softness and curves. Instead, her delicate skin covered a muscular build that took him by surprise. His beast responded, eager to couple with this strong, virile female. At the last moment he spun, using his own body to cushion their fall.

Ahhhh. Her cry rang in his ears and burrowed down into his soul. A sense of masculine pride and possessiveness filled his chest, a need so raw he couldn't deny its power over him. A thin veil of red blurred his vision, the power of the full moon on the summer solstice taking its toll on his psyche.

The spongy earth, covered in moss and small bits of grass, provided the perfect blanket of softness. Cradling her in his arms as he lay on his back, he gazed upon her masked face for the first time.

Vibrant blue eyes encased with long lashes stared back at him through the holes in her disguise. High cheekbones, flushed from her exertion, were visible beneath the edge of her mask. Although her nose was hidden behind the tip of the material, ruby red lips provided enough details to spark his imagination.

On top of him, her chest rose and fell in tune with her panted breaths. The skin on her bare arms rubbed against his chest causing the nerve endings to tingle. She struggled against him, her lithe body pressing into his crotch and his hard, hyper-sensitive cock. Apparently, she wasn't done with the chase even though he'd already caught her.

Her lips pursed and her eyes glowed with her determination, yet a slow smile curved at the corner of her mouth. His cock jerked at her play.

Using his preternatural strength, he flipped her over, encasing her in his arms. A small giggle burst from her throat. That was all the invitation he needed. He captured her lips in a bruising kiss. She wrapped her fingers in his hair and pulled him closer.

Her boldness enveloped him with a sense of euphoria. She pressed her lips against him with a force he hadn't anticipated. A surge of desire raced through his body, pumping more blood into his already engorged organ.

A soft whimper escaped her lips. He licked the soft tissue at the opening to her mouth, requesting entrance. She opened to him, and their tongues joined together. The sensation drove him mad with lust.

She relaxed under his ministrations, her arms letting go of the tension, her body conforming to his. He became aware of her blouse and the skirt covering her bottom and thighs. The annoying material needed to go.

He leaned back onto his knees, straddling her body with his legs. She ran her fingers up his arms, lighting up every nerve along the way. She stilled then through the gloves, she raked her nails down his chest. When she reached his abdominal muscles, she traced every line with a single gloved finger. His sensitive skin warmed at her touch. Behind the mask, her eyes sparkled in feminine appreciation. Her admiring gaze made him smile.

While she continued her exploration, he worked on the buttons of her blouse. His fingers fumbled with the small fasteners, and his blood pressure spiked along with his frustration. Unwilling to continue this struggle, he ripped the shirt in two.

He stilled. A seashell lined with gold hung from a chain around her throat. As pretty as it was, the bauble couldn't compare to her natural beauty. As the cool air hit her exposed skin, visible goosebumps formed, and her nipples peaked. His gaze roamed her face, taking in every visible detail outside of the mask. He wanted to rip that off, too, but held to the ritual's rules.

He ran a finger down the side of one of her breasts, circling the skin until he reached the center. He gave the delicate bud a gentle squeeze. A low moan escaped her lips, and she arched her back beneath him. Her gloved fingers dug into his biceps, increasing his desire. He captured her left hand and tugged on the mitt.

She jerked from his grasp, her index finger moving back and forth. Her pursed lips amused him, but he'd abide by her decision.

He tugged at her skirt, his beast rooting him onward. She wiggled beneath him, helping to rid herself of the confining garment. He moved down as he released her from the material, and she kicked the mini-skirt into the air. The clothing landed on the branch of a nearby tree. Her shoes slipped off her feet, leaving her naked except for her gloves and her mask.

Her laugh was like the gentle calm of a bubbling stream. He'd remember the soft twitter forever. His heart clenched. He forced the strange feelings to the back of his mind. This was all about the ritual, nothing more. He couldn't allow himself to get attached, not for her sake.

He kneeled at her feet, taking in her luscious body. His eyes riveted to the small tuft of curls at the opening of her sex. All thoughts except one fled his mind. His cock strained against his pants, eager to be freed.

His beast wanted to transform and take this female as the night demanded. He wouldn't take her that way though. He wanted to experience her in human form, but he couldn't remember why. Whether that was to maintain control of his beast or remember their time together, his fogged mind didn't know. His reason mattered not for he couldn't deny what was in his heart.

His breaths came hard and fast as he compromised, allowing the beast to rule him in human form. His beast wanted to mark her, brand her as his. A loud guttural cry broke the night air. A moment passed before he realized the sound came from his own throat.

She must've sensed his frustration, for she pulled at his belt to free him. Her fingers worked fast, the buttons of his pants undone in mere moments. His cock sprung forth, released from the torturing confines of his trousers.

She brought her hands to her lips and scooted away, onto her knees, her eyes wide. Did she fear him? Would she reject him now? He held his breath, unwilling to move even an inch.

CHAPTER 5

*L*eonna stared at the fine male specimen kneeling before her. At almost seven feet tall, he was large, even for a Stiyaha male. Muscular arms and wide shoulders tapered down to well-defined abdominal muscles. His long, firm shaft stood out from his body, as if begging for her touch. The length and breadth of him had sent her scurrying to get a better look. She wouldn't deny him, or herself.

She extended her hand and froze. Her breath caught in her throat. She still wore her gloves. If she took them off, he'd see her missing fingers and could easily identify her.

His body tensed, and his abdominal muscles clenched tight, making his cock bob in invitation.

She glanced at his face. Behind his mask, the perfect blue eyes she'd seen earlier were now flecked with bits of amber. He frowned and moistened his plump lip with his tongue.

He thinks I'm rejecting him.

He'd saved her from the other male. To deny him was the last thought on her mind. That he refused to force himself on her spoke volumes about his character. Her heart melted for this wonderful male.

She glanced at the marking, the one she'd seen as soon as he'd caught her. Three dark, concentric rings circled his shoulder—courage, conviction, and duty. Each male was born with a unique design on his body that portrayed the values most important to him. Only one male in the Keep had these lines—Prince Nicholai.

Thankful for the mask and the gloves, she could never let him know that he'd rutted with a merchant's daughter. She clamped her lips tight. She mustn't speak for he'd be able to recognize the timbre of her voice. Eager to enjoy Betram and the gift of this beautiful male, she committed herself to him, just for tonight. She wrapped her gloved hand around his shaft and squeezed. His body jerked in response and a low growl emitted from his chest.

He gripped her arms and pulled her into his embrace. His unique scent of cloves and fresh rain permeated her senses. One hand trailed up her back to the base of her neck, capturing her head in his palm. His fingers from his free hand traced over the curve of her bottom and pulled her against his hot, hard cock. A surge of desire moistened the spot between her legs.

He brought her mouth to his and gave her a gentle kiss. Under the heated conditions of Betram, his tender onslaught broke through her thin veil of control. She wanted this male, needed him inside her. Her own beast took control. A growl vibrated from her chest. He responded in kind, and their combined rumble melded together.

When he broke the kiss, she stared into his eyes. Now a deep amber, they glowed with the fire they'd built between them. With a quickness born from his beast, he removed his pants, his shoes coming off in the process.

He stalked her, crawling forward. A smile crossed his lips. With the grace born from his warrior skills, he flipped her around, and her knees dug into the soft earth. In her surprise, she latched on to his arm that wrapped around her waist.

Pressed back to front, his hard shaft lay against her inside thigh. Born of need, a soft whimper rose from her lips. He kissed the back of her ear, the nerves in the tender skin flaring from his touch. Working the fingers of his free hand down the base of her neck he lingered for a moment on the neck chain, tracing the links to the shell that rested between the creases of her cleavage. Cupping one of her heavy breasts, he tweaked her nipple with his finger.

The dampness between her legs increased. He slid his cock between her thighs, rubbing against her sensitive folds. The tip of his shaft poked through her soft hairs and emerged between her legs. She rubbed the exquisite end, enjoying how he jerked under her care.

He hissed, and the sound built the sexual tension between them. As he continued to pump back and forth, rubbing against her warm, wet flesh, she shuddered with delight. She matched his rhythm, riding him like a powerful animal. Closing her eyes, she leaned her head back against his shoulder.

Her breathing increased as she let her excitement build. He touched her clit, and she jerked. His deep chuckle resonated from his chest, and she adored how it settled into her own, stroking her on the inside. He circled her bud with care while his shaft continued to slide between her creases. The rush of blood from her head to her core brought stars to her eyes. As the orgasm crested, she cried out, unable to contain her pleasure.

He held her close, kissing the soft spot behind her ear as she calmed. His lavish attention was something she'd never experienced. She longed for more, but all they had was tonight.

She pulled away from his embrace and placed her hands on the ground. Turning to look at him, she gave him a sly smile. She arched her back, rubbing her wetness all over his shaft. His jaw tightened, and his eyes narrowed, focused solely on her.

He gripped her hips, holding her in place. Thrusting forward, he rubbed over her tender clit. She let out a hiss at the strong sensation. He pulled back and when he thrust again, he teased her by pushing against her opening. The head of his cock stretched her, but then he pulled back. He approached her again, this time going in a bit further. He slid along her folds, and she tingled on the verge of another orgasm.

His grip on her hips tightened, as if he were on the edge himself.

She arched against him, and this time he entered her all the way to the hilt. He stretched her, his fullness almost more than she could bear. He stilled, letting her adjust to his size.

When she'd accepted him, she moved in a gentle rhythm. He matched her and together they picked up speed. Faster and faster, until the sound of flesh slapping against flesh filled the night air. The shell beat against her chest to the rhythm, and, for a brief instance, she wanted the good luck to be about them.

She sensed the moment of his orgasm, blood filling his shaft just a tad more before he came. He stilled, his grip on her hips tight as he pumped inside her. His orgasm triggered hers, and she clenched him as he filled her with his semen. Pure, feminine satisfaction raced through her veins.

When they were both spent, they lay on the ground. He spooned her, cradling her butt against him. He wrapped his arm around her waist, and his breath tickled the back of her neck. A peace and contentment she'd never known filtered into her senses. She longed to stay here, in his embrace, but they had to get back. The sun would be up within the hour.

She turned in his arms to look at him. His gaze searched her face. He traced a finger down the side of her mask, over the skin on her cheek, and around her chin. His thumb stroked her bottom lip before he kissed her again.

He pulled back, and rested his head in his hand. A slow smile curved his gorgeous mouth. When he spoke, his deep voice resonated into her chest. "Tell me your name."

She tensed. Unable to speak, her vocal cords smashed together from her fear. She sat up. His marking taunted her, forcing her to face reality. He was the prince. She was a merchant's daughter. He couldn't find out who she was. As much as she'd enjoyed their time together, the memories were all they had.

She bent to kiss him one last time. Quick as she could, she stood.

"Hey, what's going on—"

She grabbed her shoes and blouse off the ground and pulled her skirt from the branches. She glanced at him. He watched her, but didn't move to stop her. Before she changed her mind, she raced into the woods and didn't look back.

CHAPTER 6

*A*s the female left through the forest, she'd taken more than just her clothes with her. Somehow, she'd taken Nicholai's heart as well. An empty feeling carved a place for itself in his gut, like a dull knife with a grudge. He closed his eyes and pinched the bridge of his nose. Her scent still lingered in the air. He relished the sweet fragrance of honey, committing it to memory. One way or another, he'd find her. He shook his head, trying to clear the beast from his mind.

He'd asked for her name. What was he thinking? To expose oneself during Betram was a direct invitation to bond. A chill rose along his arms. Thank the gods she'd refused.

Deep inside, his beast growled its discontent.

He stood and grabbed his pants. A wave of anger and frustration rose within him, and he clenched the material in his fist. With a firm thrust, he pushed his foot into the pant leg.

Snap.

He stilled. He was at a huge disadvantage with his pants around his knees, and buck naked to boot. In his musing, he hadn't heard anyone approach. The female had really turned his brain to mush.

He glanced behind him, nostrils flared, breathing in the scents around him. Gaetan's and Riktar's unique essence filled the air.

His tense muscles relaxed, and he put his other leg through the pants. As he buttoned the fly, his two companions joined him.

"Wow, what a night!" Riktar slapped Nicholai on the back. "I nailed three females. They wanted a party, who was I to refuse."

Nicholai stared at the male. Riktar wore his battle gear—black pants and a woven button-down shirt. He'd left his sword behind, just as Nicholai had, but the male's belt contained numerous blades. His dark hair, pulled back in a short queue, accentuated his status as a warrior. No wonder the females had flocked to him.

"Have a little respect." Nicholai didn't know Riktar well. Given the soldier's derogatory comment, Nicholai had no regrets about keeping his distance from him.

Riktar shot him a glance and his lip curled. "Ok, *Prince*, how'd you do?"

Nicholai shook his head. "As if I would tell you." He tied the laces on his boot. The normalcy of the process giving him a distraction.

Gaetan raised his cane. "I'm tired. I'm not in the mood for this banter." He peered at Nicholai. "Are you on your way to the portal?"

I wonder how Gaetan fared tonight. The Haelen's face had a few more lines, and the bags under his eyes seemed to drag him down. He looked tired, and that meant he'd most likely participated in the ritual.

Nicholai couldn't help smiling. "Yeah. Heading there now." The brightening sky was a good indication that the sun would be up soon.

"Good. I could use the company." Gaetan looked at Riktar and raised an eyebrow. "You coming?"

"Already did." The arrogant male's laugh echoed off the trees.

Nicholai's beast stirred. *Yes, I want to bash his brains, too.*

Sssssnap.

"Looks like our night's not quite done." Gaetan's grip on his staff tightened.

The astringent, rubbing alcohol scent of his enemy filtered into Nicholai's senses and burned his throat. He wished he had his sword. The dagger at his belt would provide some protection, but not much.

By the intensity of the smell, he guessed there were at least five Gossum. *Time to let the beast out.*

Branches in the nearby pine tree quivered with a quiet rustle. A Gossum slithered from the lowest limb, landing on its feet in the soft dirt. The hairless creature could pass for the primitive brown-skinned humans who lived in small tribes, except for shiny, black eyes and the scales that ran down its back. Muscular and powerful, the evil being exuded confidence. Its comrades joined him, and then there were five.

Time seemed to slow. Nicholai released his beast, letting the connections in his brain link together, bonding the two inextricably as one. Long hair grew over his body, covering him from head to foot. His pants and boots disappeared beneath the fur. Short, pointy tusks protruded from his jaw. The beast let out a roar.

A Gossum lashed out its long tongue, the pointed barb on the end nearly connecting with Nicholai's arm. He gripped the slippery organ and yanked the creature to him. Sharp claws dug into his leg. The blade-like nails ripped a gash from his thigh to his buttocks. The pain fueled his hatred.

Thunk. Thunk.

Out of the corner of his eye, a Gossum slid down the trunk of a tree. Two daggers, one in each eye, protruded from the dead beast. *Good throw, Riktar.*

Using the preternatural strength inherent in his kind, he picked up the creature and launched it into a nearby tree. The Gossum's body contorted into an odd position, its back broken where the creature connected with the old oak. Sticky, black goo formed on the ground, the only evidence the Gossum had ever existed.

Nicholai turned to face the remaining threat. Riktar battled one of the creatures near a boulder. The male had transformed into his beast, and at nearly nine feet, he towered over the enemy. The seasoned warrior could hold his own.

Crack. Crack.

Wood clashing against flesh and bone sent a chill over Nicholai's arms. *Gaetan!*

Farther away, two Gossum surrounded his friend. One attacked, the end of his long tongue striking Gaetan on the leg. The venom numbed the limb, forcing him to kneel, rendering his good leg as useless as his deformed one.

Nicholai froze. Fear wound its way around his muscles like a snake, holding him tight. His friend would die if he didn't help him. A fierce burn flared to life on his shoulder as his courage, along with his marking, faded.

Gaetan held both ends of his staff, using the wood as a shield against barbed tongues. One of the Gossum landed on Gaetan's back and bit him on the shoulder. The other creature continued to pelt him with its stinger.

A rage built within Nicholai, breaking his fear, and he raced to help his friend.

"*Craya!* What's wrong with you?" Riktar, having finished off the other Gossum, ran alongside Nicholai. The warrior pulled a knife from his waistband and ripped the creature off Gaetan. He stabbed it in the chest. He must've hit the heart, for the creature sagged and turned to slime.

Nicholai took out his frustration on the remaining Gossum, ripping the creature to shreds with his hands. With the threat gone, Nicholai changed back into his human form and raced to Gaetan's side.

"For the love of Lemuria, why didn't you help him sooner?"

Riktar's words dug deep into Nicholai. How could he explain his fear, his doubt, his knowledge that anyone he cared about got injured as a result of him. Tonight was confirmation, yet again, of that fact.

Nicholai helped Riktar lay the wounded Haelen on the soft ferns. Red welts from the Gossum's stingers marred his arms. Holes in his pants displayed similar marks on his legs.

Gaetan's pained moan drove a stake in Nicholai's heart. A part of him wished the Gossum had wounded him instead of Gaetan.

"Do something helpful. Call for a portal." Riktar's pursed lips and drawn eyebrows displayed his disgust.

"There's not enough energy, not with the giant gateway used for the Betram ritual. We'll have to carry him." Nicholai placed his hand under Gaetan's shoulder.

Riktar yanked the unconscious healer from Nicholai's grasp. "I'll do it."

Nicholai met Riktar's gaze. When the warrior spoke, his voice was low, concerned. "I've been on the battlefield with you many times. You've never froze like that before. What happened?"

"I don't have an answer for you." Not one he was willing to give, anyway.

Riktar shook his head and walked toward the portal, carrying their precious cargo.

Nicholai followed, his burden weighing heavy in his soul.

CHAPTER 7

*N*icholai—his strength, his soft mouth, his sensual touch— filled Leonna's mind. Her skin heated at the memory of all they'd done during the Betram ritual. Her lips were still swollen from his kisses, and she pursed them together, enjoying the slight tingle. An ache rippled through her chest. She'd never feel his mouth on her again.

She hurried through the hallways. Others on their way to their daily work filled the crowded corridor. Leonna had overslept, and she'd be late to the cart—again. She bumped into a Jixie carrying a large iron hammer, the kind used in forging the warriors' swords. He impeded her progress, and slowed her down, fueling her frustration all the more.

Laughter and loud voices preceded her as she entered the merchant's market. The vendors were already in full swing, selling their wares to the throng of customers eager to spend their hard-earned sunstones. Leonna pushed her way past a female with a young babe in her arms. The child slept, his long lashes brushing against his smooth skin. A pang of envy hit Leonna in the chest, startling her. She'd never wanted a young one before, why now? An image of

Nicholai formed in her mind, and her nipples peaked beneath her shirt. She inhaled and bit her lip.

Maman helped a customer at the cart, putting a jar filled with the golden honey into her bag. Leonna squeezed past, picked up the jars, and stacked them on the display. The customer left, leaving her alone with her mother.

"Lea, hon, you're late…" Her maman couldn't quite keep her irritation out of her voice, but her eyes held a hint of compassion.

Leonna grimaced. "I'm sorry, Maman." She didn't know what else to say. Maman was right.

"You need to be here on time. I can't get all the prep work done on my own and your father—" She waved her hand in the air.

"I know, Maman. Papa is busy at the hives. I'll do better, I promise."

Her mother's glare bore into her soul. She didn't speak, but dropped her gaze and shook her head.

Leonna's face heated. *I've got to do better. They need me.*

A female with two newbs approached the cart. The mother glanced at the different bottles, while the two young females darted around her waist. Their infectious giggles rose into the air.

"Would you like a taste?" Leonna held out three small sticks to the frazzled mother who had dark circles under her eyes.

"Yes, thank you. Here, Dottie, Denia." The female handed each child one of the testing sticks. They each dipped the end into a sample jar and put the honey in their mouths.

"Ummm…yum. Can we get some?" The taller of the two young females gripped her mother's arm as she jumped up and down.

"Yeah, please, please." The other girl joined in on the antics.

"How could I resist? Two clover honeys, please."

"Do you need the dipper?" Leonna picked up the small stick with the slatted, round ball on the end. She held the utensil out to the female Stiyaha.

The female jostled the knapsack draped over her shoulder. The weight from the bag pulled on her collarbone, leaving a red mark where the material rubbed against her skin. "No, thank you. I still have one."

Leonna handed the young mother the jars filled with yesterday's honey harvest. The female's dry hands brushed Leonna's fingers as she accepted her purchase. "Has the honey helped? You mentioned last time you wanted to try it on your scalp."

The customer glanced at Leonna's mother before focusing back on Leonna. She blinked then seemed to regain her composure. "Why, yes. The honey has helped with the dandruff, but I still suffer from the itchy skin. Any suggestions?"

"Add a bit of warm water with honey. You should be fine." Leonna raised her hand, palm forward, in the Lemurian symbol of greeting or well-being. "Stop by again, soon."

The patron nodded and turned to leave, her children already running off to the next vendor.

"That will be three stones, please." Maman's voice was pleasant, but controlled.

"Oh, I'm so sorry. I forgot!" The customer rummaged in her pack, reaching deep into the bottom.

Leonna caught maman's glance. The elder female pressed her lips together and shook her head.

How could she forget to retrieve the payment? Leonna's face heated. Her heart just wasn't into running the cart.

"Here you go." The customer handed maman three rough sunstones.

"Thank you. Enjoy the honey." Maman smiled and bowed her head in respect.

The transaction completed, the female followed her children. Leonna envied her ability to escape.

"Ugh. Lea, when will you learn?" Her mother's scolding voice was one Leonna had heard often.

"I'm sorry, Maman. I'll try harder. I promise." Leonna's need to please her mother trumped her other desires. She'd do what was necessary to help her parents, even if it meant giving up her passion.

Other patrons passed by their cart, but didn't stop. The waiting was the worst part. Leonna pictured herself sitting in front of her easel, her crushed berry paint at her side. She often made her own, searching out the best plants and berries to blend into the perfect colors. A dab of glue and the mixture reached the consistency needed for painting. She swayed to and fro, letting the euphoria take over her body like it did when she painted.

Papa walked up to the cart with a heavy bag draped over his shoulder. He placed the rough woven bag at Leonna's feet. "Well, here's the last haul for today. Would you be a dear and unload that for me?" He tugged at the brim of his hat. The hand-sewn letter 'T' emblazoned on the front caught her attention. The symbol was a testament to Lemuria and life everlasting.

Corbin strode up behind their father, along with his best friend, Blaine, who seemed a bit nervous. He glanced at her, bit his lip, and looked away.

Corbin wore his military training pants and shirt, both a deep, rich blue. He strutted in front of her, his head held high. "I won my first competition today. Short sword on the straw dummy, cut him right in half."

Papa chuckled. "That's my son." Pride radiated from his smile, as if Corbin were the best warrior in the Keep.

Leonna untied the knot surrounding the canvas bag, pulling a bit rougher than necessary on the long cord. The best warrior was the prince. Ruthless and cunning, he'd earned the reputation as the most lethal warrior. Although none knew him well, he was trusted by his fellow warriors on the battlefield. His nickname—Lone Beast or Heartbreaker. Yeah, she could attest to that one.

Memories of their evening together raced through her mind. Her skin warmed and her scent of honey permeated the air. Good thing her perfume blended in so well with their business. She couldn't believe she'd rutted with the prince. She'd never forget him, not the way he touched her, or looked at her, or how he moved in concert with her own body.

Blaine stood close by, his gaze focused on two males that leaned against the nearby flower vendor's cart. He seemed nervous, but she wasn't sure why.

"Blaine, come, let's bring Leonna in on the decision." Papa sighed, looking old and frail.

Corbin's smirk sent warning bells off in her mind, and the rope fell from her fingers. She glared at her father. "What decision?"

Papa pushed Blaine toward her. He stumbled, but caught himself on the edge of the cart. Staring at her from across the tabletop, he raised his chin, as if trying for a modicum of pride. "You and I...we... are *qithan*—intended for one another."

Her mind fogged. A shot of adrenaline coursed through her veins. Blood pounded so hard, she could hear it pumping in her ears. "Wh... what did you say?"

"We. Are. Qithan."

She refused to believe it. To become qithan was a promise to bond. Often males and females decided together to become qithan, but it wasn't unheard of for families to unite a couple to benefit the greater good of the Keep or the families themselves.

A sense of betrayal stuck in her throat. Her father had made this decision for her without saying a word. Breathing became difficult. She glanced at him, her heart aching from the deceit. He nodded. Determination lined the creases around his eyes.

"Congratulations, sis." Corbin rounded the corner of the cart and gave her a crushing hug.

She didn't know what to say. This was the last thing she wanted. She didn't love Blaine or even know him all that well. A thought crossed her mind that maybe he'd been forced into this arrangement, too.

She studied her qithan. His brown hair hung loose around his shoulders. Blue eyes the color of the rarest sunstone set her on edge. His firm lips were pursed, as if he didn't like her scrutiny. He dressed like the merchant class, his thin frame poking out from behind his tight-fitting shirt. Her qithan was nothing like Prince Nicholai. She shook her head. Why was she comparing Blaine to a male she could never have?

"Come, daughter, let him give you a token, his promise to bond." Her father placed his hands on her shoulders. He guided her around the cart, her feet moving without conscious thought.

She swallowed, which only resulted in a coughing fit. As her lungs wracked her body, she wished her soul could escape along with the air.

"He'll be a good mate, I promise. He'll help you run the cart. He's organized, never languishes in his duties, and never forgets." Her father listed off all the traits she lacked.

She wanted to crawl into a hole.

Blaine took her hands and held them in his own. His weak grip made her cringe. A male should hold her firm, with confidence—just like Nicholai did last night. Her chest constricted. She had no chance with the royal heir and needed to forget him.

"Leonna," Blaine's voice quivered, "I offer myself to you as your bonded mate. As my gift, I give you this bracelet." He held on to both of her hands with one of his. With the other, he dug into a pocket on the side of his workday pants. In his palm, a gold chain-link bracelet sparkled in the light. "Will you accept this—accept me?"

She couldn't speak. Her lips moved, but no words came out. She glanced at Papa. His pale face and tired eyes bore down on her. A quick peek at her maman with her hunched shoulders made a lump form in Leonna's throat. Her feeble parents couldn't continue to run the cart. With her brother training to become a warrior, that left her to take care of the business. Her family needed the work in order to survive and do their part in running the Keep. Despite her dream to paint, she couldn't let them down. They needed her.

She bit her lip, raised her chin and looked into Blaine's eyes. With as much courage as she could muster, she gave him her answer. "Yes, Blaine, I will become your mate." A heavy weight bore down on her soul.

Her father clapped his hands. "I already checked the council's schedule. We can get on the docket for the bonding ceremony by the end of next week."

Blaine wrapped the gold chain around her left wrist and secured the clasp. The small jewelry might as well have been a ball and chain. She closed her eyes, but couldn't stop the lone tear as it ran down her cheek.

CHAPTER 8

*N*icholai rolled onto his back and stared at the ceiling. Even the softness of his mattress and the smooth pillowcase against his head couldn't chase away his memories of last night and the Betram ritual. His thoughts volleyed between the strong, vivacious female he'd coupled with and his fear of losing Gaetan. Both vied for his attention in an internal battle of supremacy. Neither won.

He threw the sheets off and sat up. The sunstones embedded in the walls flared to light at his movement. His internal clock indicated that it was almost nightfall. He'd slept restlessly through most of the day, half-in, half-out of consciousness and dreamland, or maybe night-mare-land. With a loud exhale, he pinched the bridge of his nose.

After returning from the forest with Riktar and Gaetan, Nicholai stayed with his friend in the infirmary, helping out as best he could. Gaetan would survive, but he'd need to rest for a few days.

Nicholai inhaled, but his lungs wouldn't cooperate, as if a vise had gripped them tight. *I should've protected Gaetan.*

His mind traveled to his other distraction, one of the female variety. Even though he'd showered after returning to the Keep, the scent of honey still lingered. Against his will, his body responded. A rush of blood to his groin made him groan. As much as he tried to erase her from his mind, she was unforgettable.

After shoving himself off the bed, he opened his dresser filled with shirts, all neatly pressed and stacked. Grabbing the top one, he pulled the garment on and buttoned the fabric. Next up—black pants, boots, belt, and sword. The pants were a bit tight in the crotch. He grimaced, and adjusted himself, a bit of frustration running up his nerves.

Knock. Knock.

His scalp prickled, raising his short hairs. "Who is it?"

"Kit, I bring a message from the king."

He tensed. His father wouldn't send his personal attendant to deliver news unless the old male was in one of his moods. Great, just great. As he crossed the room, his boots scraped against the stone floor. The sound danced along his nerves like spikes.

He opened the door in a rush. The smell of fear floated in on the wake of air.

The little Jixie topped out at his belt, giving him an upfront view of just what Nicholai didn't want to show him. He could thank his honeyed female for that later, if, no when, he found her. Nicholai surreptitiously placed his hand in front of the bulge in his crotch.

The small male stared up at Nicholai, his body quivering from head to toe. "King Monroe...I mean, your father...requests your appearance in the throne room, immediately."

Yep, sounds like his father was not happy about something. He shook his head. Although he loved his father, very much, the constant pressure and expectations weighed heavy on their relationship.

Kit turned to leave, but Nicholai placed his hand on the little male's shoulder. He didn't want to scare the high strung Jixie who'd attended to his father for hundreds of years. "Kit, wait."

The Jixie peeked over his shoulder then turned to face him. "Yes, Prince?"

"Why didn't my father send a message through the sunstones?" The gems that lined the walls and ceilings of the Keep provided heat and light, but were also a means of communication.

"He did. Maybe you didn't notice." Kit bunched his shoulders and gave a chagrined smile.

Nicholai closed his eyes. Great. I'm late as well. "Tell him I'm on my way."

"Of course, absolutely. Thank you, Prince Nicholai." The small male ran down the corridor, his little feet running faster than seemed possible.

Nicholai grabbed his ring from the bedside table. As he put the jewelry on his finger, the weight of his responsibility pressed upon him.

Heat radiated from the marking on his shoulder, the circular ring for duty. The pain was a reminder of the values born into his skin at birth. His other two swirls, the one for courage and conviction were quiet. He rubbed his shoulder. On a long sigh, he headed to the throne room to deal with his father.

Nicholai stood before the king. His sire sat upon the throne, his usual attire of dark pants and a long-sleeved black shirt indicated nothing was out of the ordinary. He wore the elaborate silver crown engraved centuries ago for one of his predecessors, and the red sunstone that hung from the crest rested against his forehead. The drumming of his sunstone ring against the giant chair's armrest was the only indication that something was amiss.

A chill started at the base of Nicholai's neck and ran down his back, tingling his skin. He kneeled at the king's feet. The smell of the oak from the royal throne mixed with his mother's lavender fragrance. Her scent lingered wherever his father went, as a testament of their love. "Father. What—"

Before he could ask his question, the sound of hurried footsteps approached from behind. His gut clenched at the familiar cadence. He peered over his shoulder. *Tiernan. Perfect timing.*

"Father, I came as soon as I received the message." The king's second son bent his head to the older male, kissing him on the forehead. As usual, Tiernan wore the elegant clothing usually reserved for special occasions.

Nicholai groaned inside at his brother's display of false love. Although brothers by blood, they were as unalike as any kin could be.

"My sons." The old male's gaze bore into Nicholai before focusing on Tiernan. "I have the madness."

What? Nicholai's mind failed to comprehend what his father had said.

"The madness? How do you know?" Tiernan's voice held a hint of eagerness.

"Gaetan...he ran a test. Results were positive. The sunstones wouldn't heal me. Madness is my weakness."

"No! This isn't fair. You're too young." Nicholai clenched his fist. The madness was a memory stealer, a sickness of the brain. His father would lose track of every moment in his life, every accomplishment, every event, but most of all, he'd forget his loved ones. Impossible to identify until the flaw reared its ugly head, all Stiyaha had one weakness—one that wouldn't heal. His father's was worse than most. Many Stiyaha lived two thousand years or more, and his father's one thousandth birthday was a mere week away.

The older male rose slowly to his feet. The wooden chair creaked as if it too, had old bones. "Your mother is gathering the council. I will announce my status to them when we're through."

"Yes, father, you are much too young, you should be with us longer." Tiernan's eyes gleamed and his upper lip twitched.

A sudden coldness formed in Nicholai's chest. *Tiernan's happy about this.* Nicholai fought the sudden urge to pound his brother's head against the stone floor.

"As with anyone's flaw, I don't know how long I have before my memory fades. Once it's gone, my body will die as well, but my impending death isn't the only reason I summoned you both." Monroe's eyes moistened as he held Nicholai's attention.

Nicholai's muscles tensed.

"What I have to tell you—," the old male's voice broke, "this saddens me more than you know, my son." He placed his hand on Nicholai's shoulder.

A lump formed in Nicholai's gut.

"What is it, father?" Tiernan's voice quivered with excitement.

"Nicholai, I thought you'd put your fear behind you. I anticipated you'd become the next king." His father lowered his head and exhaled. When his gaze locked onto Nicholai's once again, he'd steeled himself. His eyes displayed his strength as king. "Gaetan...he needed you. You failed him...and me."

Nicholai took a step back. The truth in his father's words was like a dagger in his heart. "I—"

The king raised his hand. "I must select the next king. I thought this would be an easy choice, but it is not." The old leader walked to his desk where kings of the past had penned their rule.

Nicholai glanced at Tiernan. A smirk played at the corner of his brother's mouth.

A surge of anger, guilt, and frustration built in Nicholai's chest. His beast wanted to roar.

King Monroe looked at Nicholai. "Everyone has fears, but the king must be able to protect those that can't fight for themselves." His attention focused on Tiernan. "A king must be trustworthy, and put his kind before himself in all things."

Nicholai's chest constricted. His father was a strong, fair, and just king. Losing him was a blow to everyone in the Keep. Nicholai inhaled, steeling back the hard lump in his throat.

"Between the two of you, I have a difficult decision to make. Unless you can prove me wrong in my assessments, I will make my decision based on what I know." The old king peered between his two children. "I will announce the new king at my one thousandth birthday celebration in one week."

The old king clapped his hands together.

The double wide wooden doors glided open, as if they weighed nothing, not several hundred pounds of carved oak. Kit stood at the entrance, his hand extended in an invitation to exit the throne room.

"Father, I've changed. You'll see." Tiernan bowed his head to the old king. He rose and strutted out the door. On the way out, with his back to their father, Tiernan winked at Nicholai.

Nicholai clenched his teeth. How could his brother be so callous? He glanced at his father.

The elder male's skin was drawn, as if he carried a heavy weight on his shoulders. He raised his chin, ever the king, and nodded once.

Nicholai had no words for him. His father was right, he hadn't beaten his fear. He bowed in respect and walked through the throne room doors.

As he wandered down the corridor, no particular destination in mind, an old, familiar memory surfaced. One he'd played over in his head many times—one that changed him—made him so rigid he followed the rules, gave him a penchant for neatness and order, and kept others at arm's length.

Nicholai hid among the branches of an old oak tree. His best friend, Rand, hugged the trunk a few branches down. As part of the training exercises for the day, Milun, their teacher had instructed his students to hide in the trees, but not cross the river.

Nicholai snickered. He'd convinced Rand to break the rules, and his friend had reluctantly agreed.

The setting sun painted the clouds in shades of pink and orange. Nicholai's chest expanded at the beauty in the sky. As newbs, they shouldn't be out after dark, not when the Gossum roamed the forest. If caught, their disobedience would result in strict penance for the both of them. Nicholai didn't care; the view was worth the punishment.

Sssssnap. Sssssnap.

The hair on the back of Nicholai's head stood on end. He'd heard stories from the warriors about the sound of a Gossum's tongue, but in his worst nightmare, he'd never imagined a sound like this. A niggle of fear twisted in his stomach.

Rand whimpered.

Nicholai placed his finger over his lips, silencing his friend. The faint scent of astringent carried along on the breeze. Straining as far as he could reach, Nicholai offered his hand.

Rand shook his head and held on to the trunk.

Nicholai waved him on.

Rand's foot slipped off the edge of the branch, the scrape loud in the calm forest.

A Gossum appeared at the base of the tree. Its bald head reflected the waning sun, and the scales on the back of its neck flared. A long, wet tongue launched into the air, the spiked barb snapping with a loud crack. Dressed in dark clothing, the creature could almost pass as human, except for its black eyes, as dark as a moonless night sky.

Ronk. Ronk. *The creature called to its brothers with an eerie sound.*

Nicholai melded into the darkness of the upper branches, his body frozen with fear.

Rand shivered, horror painted on his face.

The creature glanced into the tree, and his black orbs gave off an eerie shine. The Gossum snapped its protracted tongue, hitting Rand in the leg.

Nicholai reached for his friend, but couldn't grasp his hand.

Rand screamed and lost his balance, plunging to the ground.

The creature attacked.

Nicholai closed his eyes, but couldn't stop the sounds that filtered into his ears. A tear ran over his cheek. The wetness drew a line down his face to mimic the scar he'd just etched onto his soul.

Screeee. A warrior's sword shrieked. Milun attacked the Gossum, his weapon glistening in the light. The creature put up a good fight, but in the end, his teacher prevailed.

"Nicholai." Milun glanced up at him.

Nicholai didn't remember climbing down the tree or the return trip to the Keep, and Milun never spoke of what happened. Nicholai's repentance came in the days and weeks ahead, in the training center and anywhere else Milun demanded. Nicholai accepted the discipline without question, eager to punish himself all the more.

CHAPTER 9

The rich fragrance of pork chops and mashed potatoes filled
the Grand Hall. This was one of Nicholai's favorite meals,
but he didn't have much of an appetite. The devastating news of his
father's illness filled his stomach like a rock. Nicholai picked up a
plate and stood in line behind an older male merchant, one he recognized, but didn't know by name. The male wore a cap with the letter
"T" engraved on the front, the symbol for Lemuria.

"Good evening, Prince." The merchant bowed his head in respect.

"To you as well," Nicholai replied.

The spoon Nicholai gripped in his hand lightened as the lump of
potatoes landed on his plate. Juice from the pork chops ran along the
edge of the mound, creating a strange-looking island, one where he
longed to escape. He shook his head and shuffled through the line.

Grief and guilt were his companions and he didn't need another,
so he sat down at a table in the corner, alone. The sunstones lining the
walls near him dimmed, as if the Keep sensed his somber mood. He
took a bite of mashed potatoes. The warm mush tasted rancid, the
bitter tang in his mouth his own doing. He placed the fork on the
plate and pushed the dish away.

The crowd filled the Grand Hall with the everyday sounds of life

—silverware tinkling against plates, laughter, spirited discussions. A high-pitched giggle caught his attention. A group of females sat nearby, deep in conversation. One had her hair tied up in a chignon. She looked his way and they locked gazes. A tinge of pink colored her neck and cheeks. As if flaunting her availability, she covered her chest with her palm, exposing her bare wrist. The other females at the table noticed her display. The tittering and gawking commenced.

He glanced away without a second thought.

At the next table, a group of males ate their fill of the evening repast. Loud chuckles and backslapping emanated from the rowdy bunch. He recognized the warriors as he'd fought alongside them many times. A part of him wanted to join the group, get to know the males, but he didn't dare. He'd kept his distance for so long, the walls around his heart were now too high to scale.

He sat alone while the world swirled around him. His reputation as the Lone Beast was well warranted. He'd preferred it that way, until last night. In one evening, his whole world had turned upside down.

Memories of the female he'd coupled with raced through his mind. The way she'd matched him in intensity and need had attracted him like a bee to her sweet nectar. He'd craved her, yet even as the beast ruled him, he'd been gentle. She was a treasure meant to be worshiped, not taken for granted.

His beast responded to the rightness of that thought. An urge to jump up and search for her raced along his nerves. If he gave in to the desire, he wouldn't stop until he found her. He ground his teeth. Deep inside, he longed for a mate and the offspring that would come from their bonding.

He'd been with a few females for a short time, but never had a serious relationship. The females wanted him for his title and the supposed benefits that entailed. If they only knew the amount of work the queen did on a daily basis, they would run for the hills.

He wiped his sweaty hands on his pants and searched the crowd. Which one was she? Would he recognize her? So many of the Stiyaha had blond hair and blue eyes. His job would not be easy. He sighed in frustration and pinched his fingers over the bridge of his nose. The real question though—what would he do once he found her?

"Son, you ok? You look a bit...pale." His mother's voice startled him.

He straightened in his seat, the images of the carefree female still wrapped around his mind. "What? Yes, yes, I'm fine. Just a bit tired." He pasted on a smile.

She studied him, as if searching for answers, her thin lips pursed. Her green eyes dug into his soul. "You've talked to your father, haven't you?"

"Mother, I'm sorry." He stood and embraced the one female who'd loved him without question. Her soothing lavender scent eased some of his tension, and he pulled back to study her.

She was as elegant as ever. Her pale green dress accented the color of her eyes. The bun at the back of her neck captured her long blond hair. The few wisps that escaped were the only sign she wasn't quite as put together as she portrayed. She quirked a smile at him. "I'm going with him, you know...your father."

A sharp pain radiated from his chest. "Mother, no—"

Shhhhhh. She placed her finger over her lips. Her smile lit up her face despite the sadness in her eyes. "Although some females stay behind after the death of their mate, it is my wish to be with him. I don't expect you to understand, not yet, anyway. Someday, when you bond to a female, *then* you will understand."

"I have no intention of bonding to a female." He'd be damned if he'd allow himself to get close enough where he'd freeze if she were ever threatened. She'd be hurt or worse, and that would be his fault. His chest tightened. Despite his longing, he'd never put a female at risk by bonding to him.

She laughed. The gentle chuckle made her smile all the more endearing. "Well, we'll see. You know, our bonding binds us together, even in death."

He glanced at her left arm, where two black bands circled her wrist. Each had a small triangle on either side, one pointing down her hand, the other pointing up her arm. These were an exact replica of his father's, except his was on his right arm. Once they'd bonded, she'd received the mirror image of his markings. The lines marked her as his mate to warn other Stiyaha males to stay away from her.

"Your father and I will meet up again on Lemuria."

Lemuria—their home planet. At death, spirits returned back to the source, back to the place from which they all came. Nicholai held his breath, afraid if he spoke his voice would waver.

"Your father's birthday is next week. Have you found a gift?" She smiled, but the usual glow in her eyes was missing.

Craya. He clenched his hand. "Not...yet." How could he think about something as trivial as a birthday present when his father had such a devastating disease?

"Let's make your father's birthday extraordinary. As special as we can, anyway." A wisp of her blond hair caught his attention. The shine and softness brought back a fond memory of his childhood when she'd read stories to him. Sitting in her lap, he'd tangled his fingers in her hair with childlike innocence. She was the only female allowed into his inner circle. He loved her deeply.

He nodded, unwilling to let his mother down. He wasn't sure he'd be successful in finding the perfect gift, if there even was such a thing given the circumstances.

"I know you'll find something wonderful. I believe in you, my son."

If only he could believe in himself.

CHAPTER 10

*L*eonna sat on the stool in front of her easel. Her legs shook. *I'm qithan.* The thought sent a chill over her arms and a knot formed in her stomach. She closed her eyes and concentrated on breathing.

Brushes swishing against canvas caught her attention. Someone coughed. A chair squeaked against the stone floor. The scent of paint and thinner, along with glue filled the room. Tension drained from her shoulders with the familiarity of it all. The artistry chamber was the one place she could come and feel at ease, not pressured to please anyone but herself. This was her little corner in the Keep. In her soul, her paintings were what defined her.

After her disastrous afternoon, she'd fled the confines of the honey cart as soon as she could. As she ran through the stalls and carts, dodging the last of the patrons, she'd heard her mother's call. *Lea, you forgot to—*

Leonna couldn't go back and face one more task. The burning need to free herself from her confining responsibilities just about broke her will. She'd kept going until she'd ended up here.

She opened her eyes and stared at the canvas. The partial painting, a young mother nursing her newborn, remained as she'd left it. The strokes were long and full, the details just beginning to take shape. Half finished, the painting reminded her of the babe she'd seen in the arms of the female she'd brushed past in the market. A longing pulled at something undefined inside her.

How long had it been since she'd come here? Weeks? She touched the dried paint, tracing the brush strokes, remembering the peace and sense of freedom that would course through her veins whenever she painted.

She picked a brush from her cylinder of painting supplies. The fine, supple goat hairs tingled her fingers and eased the ache in her chest.

"It's been a while." A low male voice broke through her thoughts.

She looked at her neighbor seated a few yard away, his own paints and brushes strewn about his feet. A toe poked through a hole in his shoe. He moved his foot and placed it around one of the stool legs. She flashed her gaze to his face.

A warm smile lit up his eyes, and he winked at her. His hands were covered in an array of colors from his work. A few splatters marred the fine hairs of his beard. "Remember me? My name's Wren."

"Oh, yes." He'd been here once or twice before. She studied his painting. "Looks like you've made progress."

The outline of trees took shape. A small waterfall cascaded over a cliff, landing on the rocks below. She admired his ability to blend the light with the shadows. "Your painting is beautiful."

A shy smile pulled at his lips. He nodded toward her canvas. "I wondered when you'd be back. I admire the way you paint. You pour all your emotions into each stroke."

"Thank you—"

He glanced over her shoulder and stiffened. His eyes widened. "Look who's here."

She turned. No, that couldn't be him, but sure enough, the male Wren had pointed out was none other than Prince Nicholai. With a quick turnabout, she faced Wren. Her heartbeat picked up speed. "What's he doing?"

Wren leaned over his canvas and gaped. "Checking out Trenden's work. Huh? Wonder why."

Her tight shoulders ached, reminding her of all she'd done with the prince two nights ago. She bit her lip.

"Everyone's staring at him. Uhhh...he's coming this way." Wren hid behind his easel.

She reached for a paintbrush, eager to appear busy. Blood pumped through her veins.

Crash.

Brushes and painting utensils scattered across the floor. *Oh, no!* She bent down to pick them up.

"Wait. He stopped at the next painter. He's scoping out his work, too. Oh, now he's looking around the room."

Murmurs from the crowd picked up. Titters of 'Prince' and 'Nicholai' were clear, even above the din.

She picked up brush after brush, trying to contain her mess. With her one good hand, she scooped as many as she could back into her container.

"He's moving faster, coming our way."

Two more brushes and she put the cup back on her short table. Her rapid breaths fueled the adrenaline that surged through her body.

"Very nice. Is this yours?" Nicholai's deep voice resonated into her chest.

As she tried to calm herself, his unique scent of cloves and rain filled her lungs. Melting on the inside, she remembered all that he was, all that he'd done to her. She refused to look at him for fear he'd recognize her.

"Y...Yes." She managed to get the words out, but they were husky, strained.

"You have a nice eye for detail. Have you other paintings?" He stepped closer to inspect her canvas. She caught a glimpse of his profile. His high cheekbones and aquiline nose exemplified his handsome features. He turned toward her.

She caught her breath. Those deep blue eyes were the ones she remembered, the ones she'd imagined in her dreams the past couple of nights. His brow furrowed, and she realized she hadn't answered his question.

"I do. Have more paintings." She turned toward her stack of completed pictures, but knocked the cup of brushes off the table.

Like twigs upon the rocks, they bounced and jogged before coming to rest on the stone floor. "I'm...sorry." She bent down to pick them up—again.

He lowered himself on one knee and picked up a handful of brushes. Just as she reached for one, he did as well. His finger ran along hers, lighting up the skin along their connection. Her scent of honey filled the air, released by her reaction to him.

He tensed. His nostrils flared. "Do I know you? You smell...familiar, like honey."

Still clutching a handful of brushes, she brought her left hand to her chest. "My family runs the honey cart. Maybe you've been there." She swallowed.

He leaned back, his scrutiny more than she could bear. As he glanced at the gold chain around her wrist, his jaw clenched, the movement clear in the skin on his cheek.

She stood and placed the brushes into the cup.

He stood as well. His brow furrowed once again when he glanced at her right hand, and the missing digits. Placing the brushes he'd collected into the bowl, he nodded. "My apologies. I must have mistaken you for someone else."

She breathed a quick sigh, and a nervous laugh escaped her lips. "Thank you for helping me with the brushes."

"Are those your other paintings?" He motioned to the stack behind her. "I'd like to see them, if you don't mind."

"Y...yes, of course." She stared at Wren. His eyes widened, and he gave her a quick nod.

Nicholai inspected each painting, flipping through them at a leisurely pace. "Do you take orders for your paintings?"

She couldn't respond around the lump in her throat. She'd never had an offer before.

He looked at her. "I'd like to commission you to paint a picture for me."

She pressed her palm against the shell necklace that lay against her chest, hidden underneath her blouse. "Sure, I can do that, I guess. What would you like?"

"A portrait of me, for my father. He's often said he'd like my picture, but I've avoided having one made. Now is the time."

Her mouth fell open, and she licked her lips. His intense focus riveted there, then drew up to her eyes. Flecks of gold swirled amongst the blue. His beast remembered, even if his human side didn't recognize her. A warmth spread through her body.

"It may take a few weeks—"

"Timing is of vital importance. You have seven days. Can you do it, or should I move on?"

His challenge should've frightened her, made her refuse his offer. Instead, she took his bait. "I can't paint during the day. You'll have to come here every night, after the carts close for the evening."

"Very well, we start tomorrow." His gaze roamed her face one last time before he turned and headed back down the row of painters.

A small thrill ran down her back. She'd get to spend time with him. A smile tugged at her mouth, but soon faded. She'd made a commitment to both her father and Blaine—one she'd honor. Her heart shattered at the reality.

CHAPTER 11

*N*icholai headed down the corridor. The sunstones in the walls brightened as he approached each doorway. Laughter, a babe in tears, strained conversations, each room contained the sounds of life in the Keep. He cared not. His mind was still fixated on the lovely female painter.

Craya. He hadn't even asked her name.

He'd thought for sure he'd found the female from the Betram ritual. Her honey scent and her pale blue eyes seemed to fit. Even his beast responded, as if she'd marked him, not the other way around. When their skin touched, the sensation racing up his arms reminded him of their lovemaking.

He shook his head. *She's not the one. This female is qithan. Besides, her hand—*

Something metal hit the stone floor, bringing him out of his musing.

Argh. "Stop! Put it down."

The smell of blood permeated Nicholai's nose.

"Hey, watch it!"

A few doors down, a brightness coming from a doorway lit up the hall. He'd ended up at the infirmary. His heart skipped a beat. *Gaetan.*

With the speed of his kind, he raced into the room. The scene before him was not what he expected.

Three warriors pinned a fourth to one of the beds. Blood pooled from the injured male's cuts and open wounds. White bone protruded from a large gash across his leg. The soldier screamed and flailed, his eyes wide, crazed. A medical tray upended. Tools scattered across the floor like miniature weapons.

Gaetan leaned against the counter, bowls and containers strewn across the surface. He picked up a large syringe filled with a green liquid.

Nicholai ran to the warriors' aid. He grabbed the wounded soldier's ankle, preventing the male from kicking out and injuring himself further.

Gaetan hobbled over, his cane resting against the wall. His gait was even more pronounced, and his face and arms still bore the red welts from the Gossum stinger.

He should've healed by now. Nicholai didn't have time to contemplate that thought for the warrior lurched from the table.

"*Craya.* Vinter! Stop." Quentin, a soldier with a red bandana tied around his bicep, spoke with a strained voice. The muscles in his arm bulged from holding down his friend.

Gaetan plunged the needle into Vinter's thigh, just above the bone break. The injured male fought for a few more seconds, then relaxed. His body jerked a few times before he closed his eyes.

Nicholai caught Quentin's gaze. "What happened?"

"Gossum ambushed us along the stream, near the giant boulder. We'd tracked a stray, but he led us upwind. Didn't see the other five until they attacked." Quentin shook his head. He made a fist, and the bandana tightened around his bicep. "They nearly killed Vinter. We managed to battle our way back to the portal, but not before he'd sustained injuries."

The Haelen glanced at his patient. "He needs his rest, and I need time alone to fix his leg before it heals this way." Gaetan furrowed his eyebrows and glared at each of the males. "The rest of you don't look too bad, you'll heal on your own." He raised his hand and shooed the warriors out of the room.

Nicholai refused to leave. Now that he was here, he needed to apologize to his friend.

Gaetan raised an eyebrow. "That includes you."

Nicholai sighed and shook his head. What did he expect, a warm hug? "Seems to me, you could use the help."

The healer shrugged and hobbled over to his cane. Gripping the handle, he leaned on the stick for support. His back to Nicholai, the male shoulder's slumped forward, but he was only a few years older than Nicholai. He picked up a tray with bandages, an assortment of medical instruments, and a large orange sunstone. As he walked back to Vinter, the tray wobbled in his hand. The rock shimmied against the carved stone tray, and the sound reminded Nicholai of chattering teeth.

"Let me get that for you." Nicholai scooped up the platter and placed it next to Vinter.

The injured male let out a loud snore.

Gaetan stood next to Vinter's damaged leg and scrutinized the damage. "He's lucky he didn't rupture his femoral artery." Gaetan ran his hand over the torn flesh. A fresh trickle of blood oozed from the injury.

"Well, if you're going to stay, you can help." Gaetan held out his hand. "Scissors."

Nicholai handed the Haelen a long pair of clippers. The pointed ends glimmered in the light. A wave of guilt crashed over Nicholai and his stomach hardened. He should've helped Gaetan. What could he possibly say to the male? He thought an apology would be easy, but he'd thought wrong.

The material surrounding the wound fell to the side under the shears' sharp blades. Gaetan scooted to the end of the table and gripped the male's foot in his hand. With a quick jerk, the bone disappeared beneath the skin.

"Rock." Once again, Gaetan held out his hand, but he wouldn't look at Nicholai.

Nicholai handed the orange crystal to his friend. The stone's heavy weight matched the lump in his gut.

Gaetan held the stone over the break. A glow emanated from the sunstone, casting a strange shadow over Gaetan's face. The Haelen's features appeared gaunt in the faint light.

The radiance from the stone went out as quickly as it had started. Red, mottled flesh replaced the gaping wound. A scab formed and would fall off in a matter of hours. The skin would scar then heal completely in a few days as if the injury had never occurred. The warrior would fight again soon.

Nicholai swallowed. "Gaetan—"

"Bandage." Gaetan held out his hand, but this time he met Nicholai's gaze.

"I'm sorry. I…" Nicholai's chest constricted, cutting off any further words. He didn't know what else to say.

Gaetan focused on his work. "I trusted you." His eyes bore into Nicholai's soul. "I—"

"I know. I froze. I'm sorry." The memories of the Gossum's tongue connecting with Gaetan's arms, legs, face—the weight of Nicholai's weakness bore down on him.

Gaetan returned his attention to his task. "We've talked about this before. I thought you'd beaten those demons." Gaetan paused. His hands rested against the male's legs, the remaining bunch of dressing still in his palm. He glanced at Nicholai.

"I did, too." Nicholai could barely get the words out. "If I could trade places with you…absorb those injuries, I would."

Gaetan clipped the bandage in place then grabbed his cane. He came closer, his pale blue eyes carrying a hint of forgiveness. "No need. I'm fine, but you need to figure this out before someone who really matters to you gets hurt."

Gaetan's words hit home. A fleeting image crossed Nicholai's mind —that of a female with blue eyes hiding behind a mask. His gut clenched like he'd been punched. Maybe he was better off not knowing her identity. Correction, maybe she was.

CHAPTER 12

*L*eonna tucked the sheet under the mattress and fluffed her pillow. As she pulled the warm quilt over her bed, she relished in the feel of the soft fabric. Despite its comfort, she hadn't slept well. Visions of Nicholai and the intensity of his gaze had kept her awake for hours. His beast had recognized her, both by sight and smell.

She stroked the remaining finger on her right hand. Her black gloves had hidden the missing digits well during the Betram ritual. Tonight, she'd wanted to admit to Nicholai that she was the one, but what good would come of it? She glanced at the bracelet around her left wrist. The gold chain was a constant reminder of her upcoming commitment. Her vision blurred as tears gathered, and the red and blue pattern of her bedspread melded into an odd purple. She bit her lip, unwilling to give in.

Her stomach rumbled—time for the morning repast. She slipped on her well-worn shoes and grabbed a ribbon from her dresser. The sunstones in her room dimmed as she entered her family's main chamber.

Papa sat at the small wooden table. He dipped his spoon into a cut grapefruit, and juice squirted onto his clothes. He chuckled, wiping away the liquid with his palm. Leonna slid into a chair next to him. The pictures of her and Corbin she'd painted a few years ago hung against the stone wall. She'd grown up a lot since then, both of them had.

Wrapping her long hair in the ribbon, she studied him. "Good morning, Papa. Not going to the Grand Hall for repast?"

"Don't have time. Need to get to the hives." Papa peered at her and raised an eyebrow. "You were out late."

Excited about seeing Nicholai and painting for him had inspired her to sketch, so she'd stayed late in the artistry chamber. She often sketched before painting. The activity helped flesh out her ideas before committing them to canvas. At the memory, remnants of the euphoria coursed through her veins, filling her with happiness. A smile tugged at her lips, and she gave in, letting the warm feeling raise her spirit. She felt taller, bigger, stronger than she'd felt in a long time. Eager to tell him about her commission to paint for the prince, she took in a large breath. "Papa, last night—"

"Last night, you left your mother to handle the clean-up. When are you going to become more responsible?" His flat tone conveyed his displeasure.

Her elation deflated in an instant. "I—I'm sorry, father. I…"

"Riordan, let her be." Maman entered the room, her hands still fiddling with the pins in her hair.

"Pia, she needs to learn—"

"Agreed, but we don't need to attack her with responsibilities first thing in the morning, do we?" Maman placed her hand against Leonna's back and rubbed her shoulder.

Leonna blinked rapidly to stave off the wave of tears that hit her full force.

Her father wiped his mouth with his napkin and threw the cloth on the table. "I'm heading out. Lots to do." He stood, and his eyes widened. His body swayed as if he were on a boat in a rough sea.

A kernel of dread formed in Leonna's stomach. She leapt to her feet. "Papa!"

Both she and her mother reached him just as his knees buckled. He outweighed them both, but with their combined strength they managed to get him back into his chair. The rickety seat groaned under his weight.

"Riordan, what is it?" Anxiety filled her mother's voice and mirrored the concern Leonna felt in her own chest.

He rubbed his pale face, his eyes focused on a spot over Leonna's shoulder. "Nothing, it's nothing. I stood up too quickly. Just a little light-headed."

"Papa, we should take you to see Gaetan."

"No!" He slapped his palm on the table. "I've already visited the Haelen. There isn't anything he can do."

Leonna flinched.

He let out a long breath. "I'm fine, really."

Leonna glanced at Maman. They locked gazes. She could tell by the doubt in her mother's eyes that she didn't believe him either, but based on prior experience, there was no getting through to him.

Leonna stepped back, and her mother did likewise. Leonna's hands shook. The lines in his face and his pale skin, made her want to cry. She couldn't imagine anything happening to her father.

He stood. His fingers gripped the edge of the table for a moment, as if he needed the extra support for balance. He looked hard at her. "Meet me at the cart after you've eaten."

He meant business. "Yes, Papa." She bowed in respect.

He reached to open the door.

Knock. Knock.

He flinched at the noise, but turned the knob. "Ah, Blaine, good morning to you. Welcome, come in." He spread his hand wide, beckoning her qithan into their home.

Her heart skipped a beat, and not in a good way. Her mother's comforting hand squeezed Leonna's arm.

Blaine strode into the room. He held a bouquet of red roses. The sickly sweet smell of the flowers permeated her senses. He lacked that special connecting spark in his eyes. She didn't feel any sort of attraction to him, not like she did to Nicholai, and the difference was like a splash of cold water on her soul.

"H…Hello, Leonna. These are for you." He extended his arm. The flowers shimmied in his grasp as if he was unsure about her reaction.

Against her will, her desire to please kicked in. She took the flowers from him and glanced at the ground. "Thank you."

She turned to get a vase, eager to escape both males in her life.

"Well, then, I'll be off." Her father's voice had an extra lilt. The door shut with a soft click.

Leonna cringed. She pulled out a vase from a nearby cabinet, filled it with water from their drinking pitcher, and placed the beautiful, yet depressing, flowers on the center of the table.

"May I walk you to your cart today?" His voice squeaked on the last word.

She wanted to run, hide, do anything but spend time with this male, but after the episode with her father, the reality that Blaine was to be part of her future weighed on her.

"Sure." Somehow, she managed to force the word out.

With tentative steps, she approached him. He held out his arm, and she wrapped her hand in the crook of his elbow.

"Leonna, I'll meet you there. I forgot my shawl in my room." The soft padding of her mother's feet receded.

She peeked at Blaine. He stared at her mouth. With a sense of dread, she licked her lips. He cupped her head with his free hand and kissed her.

No. Sparks. Whatsoever.

Instead, a weird sense—like kissing her brother crossed her mind. *Eww.*

He released her and cleared his throat. "We should get going. The carts open soon. We both have responsibilities to our families."

A thought occurred to her that maybe, just maybe, he had been coerced into this arrangement as much as she had. She wanted to ask him, but maman reappeared in the room. The opportunity was lost.

As they exited her family chamber, a strange sensation, like tentacles from a giant octopus, clamped around her chest, taking her breath away. She felt trapped and hopeless, with nowhere else to go.

CHAPTER 13

*L*eonna picked at her food. The carrots and corn on the cob blended together as tears formed in her eyes. She fisted her hand and blinked, willing herself to take control, to not let a single drop spill from her lashes.

A group of warriors at a nearby table caught her attention. They laughed and chatted among themselves, their plates loaded with the pulled pork and vegetables from the evening repast. One male had a marking that ran from his elbow up his arm until the line disappeared under his shirtsleeve. She wondered if his mark looked anything like Nicholai's.

She inhaled at the thought. *I'm qithan. I shouldn't think about Nicholai.* But that was all she wanted to do. She bit the inside of her cheek, and a new round of tears threatened.

The line of Stiyaha in front of the food tables wound into the hallway. Good thing she'd arrived early. She needed to eat and get to the artistry chamber to meet the Prince. A lump formed in her throat, and she couldn't swallow the bit of carrot in her mouth. She held her breath and forced herself to calm down. At last, she swallowed, but the effort left her with a bitter tang in her mouth.

Chantel approached with a full plate. Her face beamed, and her mouth curved into a mischievous grin. As she closed the distance, her smile faltered. "Why are you sitting over here by yourself?" Her best friend snuggled beside her on the bench and ran her hand up Leonna's arm, but the friendly gesture didn't ease the ache in her heart.

"Chanty...I'm qithan." Leonna raised her arm, and the bracelet dangled from her wrist like a rope, one attached to a male she didn't love.

Chantel's quick breath gave away her surprise. "....and that explains your happy mood, right?" Chantel wrapped her into a soft embrace. "What can I do?"

"Nothing. Just...nothing." The heat and aroma from the pulled pork didn't help Leonna's stomach. She clamped her mouth shut to hold back the nausea rising in her throat.

Chantel pulled back and stared into Leonna's eyes. "Who is he? Do I know him? Do you even like him?"

So many questions Leonna wasn't sure how to respond, so she shook her head.

"Then why are you qithan with him?" Her friend tightened her lips and gave her a troubled glare.

"It's complicated."

"That's not an answer. Please tell me...or I will tickle you until you do."

A short laugh burst from Leonna. Her friend always had a way of raising her spirits. A small smile pulled at her lips, and a bit of her tension abated.

"I made you laugh. That's a start." Chantel pushed her uneaten food away and stood. "Let's walk—get the blood flowing. It'll do you good." She stood and grabbed Leonna's hand.

Leonna went along, suddenly eager to escape the Grand Hall, now filled with so many of the Keep's residents. As they walked down the corridor, their pace picked up. Fresh air filled her lungs, providing oxygen for her muscles and her brain. Her friend was right—she felt better.

"Now, tell me what happened." Chantel's tone was encouraging, yet demanding.

"My father…he selected Blaine as my mate." As Leonna said the words, the chain around her wrist grew heavier.

"Blaine? I must be wrong, but I thought he preferred—"

Adrenaline coursed through her veins as a deep desire to let it all out hit Leonna. "Papa doesn't trust me to run the honey cart on my own. He thinks I'm too impulsive and disorganized." Leonna took a big breath. "He grows feebler each day…and my mother, what with her bent back, she can't run the wagon. So, he selected Blaine to help me. He didn't even ask what I wanted. He—" The floodgates burst and the tears flowed. She inhaled to prevent the wail that threatened to escape.

Chantel wrapped Leonna in a firm embrace. "I'm so sorry. Why don't you tell him what you want?"

Leonna's body hitched as she tried to control her sobs. A vision of Nicholai crossed her mind, but the thought of being with the prince was futile, so she focused on her other love—art. That wasn't a viable option for a living. She used to be a fabulous painter, one with the promise of a great career. Ever since the accident, her paintings just didn't quite have that same spark, the same beauty.

An unwanted memory coiled itself from the depths of her brain. As a newb, she'd run off from her father and their honey cart, excited to paint. As she ran down the market aisle, an older female appeared in her path. Unable to stop, Leonna crashed into her and both fell to the stone floor. Pinned underneath the other female, Leonna couldn't move, her arms sprawled out in front of her. A nearby vendor's cart rolled down the aisle. Before she could scream a warning, the cart's wheels ran over her hand, cutting off three of her fingers. As much as Gaetan had tried, his healing stones couldn't reattach the severed digits. Even today, the creak of cart wheels sent goosebumps along her arms.

Leonna pulled away from her friend and looked into Chantel's eyes. "I have a responsibility to my parents to run the honey cart. It's our family legacy—our contribution to the Keep. What I want doesn't matter."

"Not true. What you want *does* matter." Chantel traced her finger over Leonna's hair. "Oh, honey, why you can't see that I'll never understand."

"Thank you for helping me work through this, but I have to get to the artistry chamber. I'm meeting someone for a painting."

Chantel's gaze roamed Leonna's face, as if she evaluated whether she was ready to let her go. She glanced at the stone floor and stepped back. "Okay. I'd love to see the picture when you're done. I'm sure the painting will be beautiful."

Leonna's muscles relaxed. She pulled Chantel into a quick embrace. "You're a good friend, Chanty."

CHAPTER 14

There she was. The female he'd commissioned to paint his portrait. She brushed a stroke of paint over her canvas, the movement sensual, beautiful. That she used her damaged hand was remarkable. Her thumb and index finger grasped the brush with ease. Mesmerized, he could gaze upon her face for not just hours, but days on end. As he walked past the other artists in the room, none caught his attention, not like this female.

Nicholai's body responded as if he knew her, as if she was the one he'd been with during the Betram ritual. But she was not. As a qithan female, she wouldn't have been allowed to participate. Then, why did he respond to her this way? He ground his teeth. The last time they'd talked, he'd failed to get her name. He would rectify that immediately.

Her back to him, she didn't appear to notice his approach. He gazed upon her fine, blond hair. The stands fell down her back. The tips graced the top of her rounded behind. He had a sudden urge to get close, introduce himself by showing her what she did to him. That was inappropriate, but his beast liked the idea.

Not wanting to startle her, he stepped past her so that he'd be in her line of sight. She jumped anyway, and a drop of red paint from her brush landed on her cheek. The bright spot made her all the more delectable. She didn't seem to notice.

Her eyes widened.

"Oh, you're here." She blushed a bright shade of pink that blended well with the dab of paint. He longed to wipe it away, but contained his desire.

"Yes, as promised." He couldn't help the smile that tugged at his lip. She brought that out in him. The smile overtook him and turned into a full grin.

If possible, her cheeks colored even darker shade of pink, and his chest expanded from the warmth she exuded.

"I have a fresh canvas." She removed the painting she'd been working on and pulled a white board from her stack. "It's brand new, and—"

"What's your name?" A burning desire to know ate at him.

She bit her lip.

A warmth spread into his groin. He wanted to nibble her lip as well.

"Leonna."

"Leonna." The way her name rolled around on his tongue was like a gentle caress. So, he said her name again. "Leonna. What a beautiful name. I am Nicholai."

"I know." She stiffened. "I mean...I recognize you, Nicholai... you're the prince. Everyone knows who you are."

Hearing his name come from her lips made his beast sit up and take notice. If it wasn't for the qithan bracelet and her misshapen hand, he'd swear she was the one from the Betram ritual.

The red dot of paint on her cheek turned lighter as it dried along the edges. He couldn't wait any longer. With the back of his finger, he wiped her cheek. His skin lit up at the contact.

She inhaled, and her lips parted. Her mouth was an open invitation. An overwhelming urge to kiss her ran along his nerves like a raw current. He balled his other hand into a fist. His beast roared at the injustice.

"Paint splatter." He held up his finger, now red with the oil. "I couldn't leave it there to mar your pretty face."

She held his look, her eyes darting back and forth, as if she might be trying to understand his intentions. She broke eye contact, and offered her chair to him. "Please, sit here."

He did as she indicated. The old wooden chair creaked under his weight. He stiffened, worried for a moment that the relic would break. When it didn't, he relaxed. Intrigued, he sat back and watched as she prepared for her work, gathering her brushes and paints around her workstation. She had a small dimple in her cheek that puckered when she smiled.

"Leonna, do you paint often?" He enjoyed the sound of her name and made a mental note to say it often.

She glanced at him. There was a hint of disappointment in the curve of her mouth. "Not as much as I'd like." She studied him. A small, admiring gleam flashed in her eyes, but then the twinkle disappeared. "Turn to the left a bit, please."

He chuckled to himself and cooperated. "Like this?"

She furrowed her brow. "A little less, more toward me."

He complied. "So, when you're not painting, what occupies your time?"

She stilled for a moment, a paintbrush in her hand. "I help my family in the market."

Flat. Emotionless. Her tone said what her words did not.

"You mentioned that your family ran the honey cart. I have a new penchant for the bees' endeavors." He chuckled just to see her reaction.

She blushed, her skin turning pink once again. Placing her finger over her lip, she whispered. "I need silence to create my best work."

Whether she teased him on purpose or not, his body responded anyway. As his heartbeat picked up its pace, blood rushed through his veins. His pants became uncomfortable. He readjusted himself in the seat, hoping she didn't pick up on his discomfort.

A shy, knowing smile crossed her face, but she didn't comment. Instead, she put the paintbrush back in the cup and pulled out a piece of paper and a charcoal pencil. "I need to sketch you first before I put the pigment to canvas."

She concentrated on her work. Despite the bustle and noise of the crowd and other artists around them, the scratching of pencil to paper was all he heard. Curiosity got the better of him, and he peeked at the paper. She moved it out of the way. Her pursed lips and vibrant eyes told him to stay put.

She moved with such grace. Her body swayed with the movements of her hand, as if she danced to her own special tune. Each time she glanced at him, she captured a little bit more of his soul.

A cold draft blew across his arms. She looked over his head. A sense of unease prickled his skin. He turned to face—

"Well, well. I can't believe my eyes." Tiernan lifted the corner of his mouth in a smug smile. "You're finally getting your portrait done." He walked closer to Leonna and stared at the sketch.

A strange need to protect reared up inside Nicholai. *Get away from her.*

"Eh, not bad, I suppose. Anyone would have a difficult time with your face." Tiernan smirked.

Nicholai stood and gripped his brother's arm. "Apologize. Now."

"To you? Never."

"Not me. Leonna."

"Ah, Leonna is her name, is it?" Tiernan yanked his arm out of Nicholai's grasp. His gaze raked from her head to her toes. "You're a pretty one, I'll give you that."

Nicholai's beast roared. He couldn't take it any longer and pushed Tiernan out of the way. Stumbling, Tiernan hit the easel of the artist next to Leonna.

Paint spilled, brushes flew through the air like small, bushy-tailed birds, and the wooden frame surrounding the canvas broke apart. The other patrons and artists scattered, their *oohs* and *aahs* loud in the now quiet room. Tiernan narrowed his eyes, his lips pressed tight. His neck and cheeks reddened.

In all the commotion, Nicholai had grabbed Leonna, cradling her to his body. With his arm wrapped around her waist, the sensation that this was where she belonged couldn't be denied. She leaned against him, pressing her bottom into his crotch. His body responded as blood rushed to his groin. He expected her to pull away, but she didn't move. A possessiveness like he'd never experienced before welled up inside him. *Mine.*

"Do not insult her again." Nicholai's breath came out in great huffs.

Tiernan stood slowly. His glare never left Nicholai's. "Watch yourself, *brother*. Father is going to make me king. When he does, you'll regret this little episode."

"We'll see about that." Nicholai moved Leonna behind him, away from his ever-loving brother.

Tiernan spat on the stone floor. Spittle splashed against Nicholai's boot. He wouldn't take the bait. As much as he wanted to hit the male, a fight with his brother was not the answer.

Tiernan laughed, straightened his shirt and walked away.

Nicholai faced Leonna, maintaining contact with her by stroking her hair. Her pale blue eyes penetrated deep into his soul. "Thank you, Nicholai."

As she said his name, his confused mind didn't know how to interpret what his body told him. She seemed like the female from the Betram ritual, but she couldn't be. His marking for duty blazed to life on his shoulder. The burn reminded him that she was qithan. Unwilling to cross that line, he couldn't stay here, not with his beast raging to claim her.

"I have to go." He stepped back. The loss of contact left him cold. "I'll return again tomorrow night." He didn't wait for her response, but turned and walked away.

CHAPTER 15

*N*icholai landed on the floor in the Portal Navigation Center. Bent into a crouch, the cold stone floor was a welcome relief on his warm palms. He exhaled, his breath still visible in the mist that drifted in through the opening. The smell of pine and wet leaves mixed with the scent of blood. A chill settled over his shoulders and ran down his arms.

The battle with the Gossum had left several warriors with injuries, some minor, some requiring a trip to the infirmary. His brother had made a terrible mistake—he'd missed a Gossum's shed skin. Nicholai had spotted the thin membrane hanging from a branch. He'd pointed the nasty remnants out to Tiernan who had taken the lead, but then, the Gossum dropped from the trees, surprising the group of soldiers.

As Nicholai rose, the cacophony of chaos rang in his ears. A warrior hustled by, his arm wrapped around the shoulder of another, helping the wounded male into the hallway. The good news—the infirmary was only a few doors down.

Rin swirled his hand over the *porte stanen* and the portal closed, shutting out the forest, along with their enemy. The little Jixie rubbed his hands together, his brow furrowing, as if his fingers hurt. He glanced at Nicholai and a welcome smile graced his features.

A strong hand gripped Nicholai's shoulder. "What were you thinking?"

Nicholai swiveled his head. Tiernan's green eyes bore into him.

Nicholai tensed. "Are you accusing me of something?" After the episode several days ago between Tiernan and Leonna, Nicholai couldn't help but antagonize his brother.

One of the nearby warriors glanced in their direction. A line of blood stained his shirt above his chest.

"You should've warned us about the Gossum?" Tiernan's jaw flexed.

This wasn't the first time his brother had accused him of something to protect his own hide. "Care to explain yourself?"

"There was a Gossum skin hanging in a tree. You should've warned us."

Several of the soldiers stopped unloading their weapons and turned to listen.

Nicholai wouldn't call out his brother's deception in front of the other males. Instead, he raised his chin and threw back his shoulders. "Irrelevant. We should've defeated them regardless of who struck first."

Tiernan scanned the room, his eyes locking with Alden and Macion, his two closest friends. "After what happened to Gaetan, and now this," he waved his hand toward a couple of injured warriors, "I refuse to go on patrol with you again."

Nicholai's stomach knotted. "As you wish. I care not." He turned to leave, finished with his brother's antics.

Tiernan's laugh made him halt.

Nicholai moved in a slow circle to face his brother.

Tiernan wiped a dagger's blade across his dark pants. The wet streak of the Gossum's black goo reflected the light from the sunstones. He held up the dagger and studied the blade as he twisted it in his hand. "What a fine piece of work, don't you think?"

His gaze lifted to Nicholai and a haughty smile crossed his face. "I've initiated the weapon on one of the Gossum tonight. I think father will be pleased, don't you?"

The gilded handle contained three rare, red sunstones, and the blade flashed in the light. It was a magnificent piece.

Nicholai held his composure and shrugged. "I'm sure he will sleep with the weapon under his pillow."

Tiernan smirked. "And what, eldest son, are you giving the king for his special birthday?"

The warriors that needed medical attention were gone, leaving only a handful of males. The deafening quiet in the room was like a loud roar in Nicholai's ears.

Nicholai gritted his teeth. Although he hadn't kept the painting a secret, to speak of the picture here, in front of the warriors, didn't sit well with him. The painting was a private, personal gift, not something to boast about. The silence continued.

"Tiernan! If yer done here, git out of my portal room." Rin walked in front of Tiernan and placed his hands on his hips.

The top of Rin's head was even with Tiernan's belt. A simple push from Tiernan and the little Jixie would find himself on the ground. That Rin would stand up for Nicholai floored him and a well of respect built inside his chest.

"That's okay, Rin," Nicholai placed his hand on the male's shoulder, "we're done here."

Nicholai sighed. Since the day Tiernan was born, his brother had tried to best him in everything—from battle training to schoolwork to friends—anything to gain an upper hand. Despite all his misgivings, Nicholai still cared for his brother. "My gift matters not. I'm sure father will cherish the dagger."

"Here, have a closer look." Tiernan approached Nicholai, the blade gripped tight in his hand.

Nicholai tensed. Before he could react, Tiernan sliced the blade at his face. A burning sensation pulsed from his lip. The taste of blood filled his mouth.

Nicholai grabbed Tiernan's wrist, the dagger held in the small space between them.

"Oh, my apologies, brother. Seems to me, I nicked you." Tiernan's eyes widened in mock surprise. "Your lip is bleeding."

Nicholai shoved Tiernan's hand away and stepped back. He wiped his mouth. Blood coated his fingers. A wave of heat made him break into a sweat. He clenched his jaw to hold back his rage. When he spoke, he fought to control his voice, keeping it low and even. "Never. Do. That. Again."

"Oh, brother, are you threatening me? In front of these warriors?" Tiernan raised his eyebrows.

Nicholai leaned toward his only sibling. "If I had threatened you, you'd already be dead."

His brother's smile faded from his face. He took a step back.

A snicker erupted from one of the nearby males.

Nicholai shook his head. "Tiernan, I'm not the enemy."

Tiernan's tight face and pursed lips spoke volumes.

A deep regret knotted itself in Nicholai's gut. Why did he keep trying with his brother? He glanced at the other males, nodded, and left the room. Too bad he couldn't shed his brother's transgression as easily.

CHAPTER 16

$\mathcal{N}$icholai fidgeted in his chair, and the heel of his boot beat out a steady rhythm against the stone floor. He'd come to the artistry chamber every evening for the past six nights, as much to see Leonna as to have his portrait painted. Working on her, he'd encouraged her to talk. She'd eventually opened up, telling him about her parents and her brother. Never once had she mentioned her qithan.

The swish of her paintbrush matched her delicate movements. To watch her was a joy and a privilege. She had an air of the unexpected about her that called to him, to his controlling, have-to-have-every-thing-in-its-place personality. Her presence filled in the empty spot in his soul. His attraction to her had grown as much from her quick wit as her beautiful smile.

The painting would be finished tonight, just in time for his father's birthday tomorrow. A lump of dread settled itself into his stomach. He'd have no reason to see her again.

Her gaze roamed his face, her eyes focused. She dipped her brush in yellow paint, the tips wet with the stain. "Nicholai."

He sat taller, the cadence of her voice playing along his nerves like fingers on a stringed instrument. She owned him, whether she knew it or not.

"Tilt your chin down. Yes, like that."

She swayed to and fro as she painted. Caught up in her dance, he could watch her for eternity.

A female approached, one of the few left in the room at this late hour, a heavy canvas bag over her shoulder. Raising an eyebrow, she glanced between him and the canvas. Her lip quirked at the corner, and she nodded. "Excellent likeness."

"Thank you." Leonna gave her a quick smile, but didn't stop her rhythm.

The female continued on her way, past the few remaining artists and crafters.

"When can I see?" A desire to jump from his seat and look at the painting made his legs twitch. She'd kept the portrait from him, citing her artist right to keep the picture to herself until completed.

She caught his gaze. "Not yet." A smile curled her lip.

He chuckled.

She stopped, her brush held in mid-air. Her eyebrows furrowed for a moment, then relaxed. "I've been meaning to ask—how did you get that cut on your lip?"

His tongue ran over the gash. She focused on his mouth, her pupils dilating, giving away her desire. A rush of adrenaline sent blood screaming into his veins. He clenched his jaw, unwilling to let her see how much she affected him.

He couldn't deny his attraction to her, his need to be with her, but he couldn't risk getting too close. *Craya.* Maybe he'd already passed the point of no return. A tendril of fear tittered over his nerves.

"I received the nick earlier coming back from patrol. It matters not." He shrugged. Given his fast metabolism, the laceration would heal in a few hours as if he'd never been cut.

Her eyes widened. "Your reputation as a great warrior precedes you."

"My team…we do our best to protect the Keep."

"I can imagine, but others say…" She bit her lip.

He'd heard the rumors, too, the ones about his hesitation to help Gaetan. "That I can't be trusted?"

She looked at the ground for a moment, then returned her attention to him. Her mouth pressed together into a thin line. "I don't believe that. I won't."

His skin tingled. Her unexpected words soothed him. She believed in him. Too bad he didn't believe in himself. He closed his eyes and pinched the bridge of his nose. "Maybe you should. You don't know me."

She put the brush in a small container filled with a dark liquid. As she moved toward him, she kneeled down, and placed a hand on his arm. Her soft touch on his skin tingled his nerves. When she spoke, her words were soft, but forceful. "But I do. Tell me why you don't."

Before he could hold his tongue, the words slipped from his lips. "Because I'm a danger to anyone I care about."

"Really? Why?"

She didn't know how her questions scraped his wound. He stared into her vibrant blue eyes and lost his soul. His need to keep his weakness to himself wasn't as strong as his desire to answer her. "I lost a friend when I was a child. He was in danger, and I froze. He died because of me."

She studied him. He steeled himself for her rejection. Instead, she smiled and placed her hand on his woven shirt, over his marking. "Your swirls are there for a reason. I have no doubt of your courage."

His stomach contracted as if the organ had turned upside down. He opened his mouth, but no words came out.

She gave him her winning smile, the one he'd grown to love. As she moved to stand, a gold chain slid out from underneath her blouse. His attention riveted on the delicate thread. A jolt of recognition flashed through his mind. Before he could think, he placed his finger under the chain and pulled.

A small bauble emerged from beneath her blouse. As he focused on the shell with the gold inlay, he inhaled and held his breath.

She pulled back, clasping her necklace in her hand. Her wide eyes searched his, as if uncertain of his reaction.

Eyes locked on her, he stood and closed the distance between them. "It *is* you. I should've trusted my instincts." As if he had the right, he stroked the fine strands of her golden hair from her head to her waist. *Mine.* His shoulder burned as both his marking for conviction and duty blazed to life. The contradiction made him pause. How could she be his when she was qithan to another male?

He touched the gold band surrounding her left wrist. When he spoke, the words came out harsher than he intended. "Tell me about him."

His words weren't a question, but a statement, a demand from a male with a stake in the game. Her mouth dry, Leonna couldn't respond. The world around her dimmed, and her heightened senses became aware of this strong, virile male. His scent of cloves and rain wrapped around her like a warm blanket. Without thought, she ran her hands over his bare arms. The skin-on-skin contact tingled her fingers, and sent a shiver of excitement to her core.

He growled, the sound low and deep in his chest. Pulling her into his arms, he cradled her head in his large hand. With his free hand he ran his fingers down her back, coming to rest at her hip. His arm wrapped around her waist, and he captured her in his embrace. A warm wetness dampened her panties, and her own scent filled the air.

He massaged the back of her scalp with talented fingers, turning her to putty. She glanced into his eyes, and the amber that flickered there spoke louder than words. A new wave of desire hit her, and she licked her lips. He bent his head toward her, caressing her lips with his. The tender, sensual kiss broke her resolve, and she parted her mouth in invitation.

He took her up on her offer, and their tongues joined together. She tasted the slight bitter tang of blood, remnants from the gash on his lip. Did it cause him pain? He didn't seem to mind, his mouth devouring hers with a force she couldn't escape. Memories of Betram and their coupling raced through her mind. She pressed into him, her breasts pushing against hard muscles hidden beneath his shirt. His hand moved from her waist to her bottom, pressing her against his erection.

A soft moan escaped her lips.

He growled a sound of pure frustration. Releasing her from their embrace, he rested his forehead against hers. His quick pants were evidence of his own desire. "Does he kiss you like that?"

She tensed. The gold chain on her wrist pulled her down like a shackle. She pulled back to look at him.

Gold flecks mixed with the blue in his eyes. He studied her, waiting for her answer.

"N—N—no! Nothing like that."

"You've known all along it was me, didn't you?" His brows furrowed. "How?"

"You weren't wearing your shirt..." Her gaze darted to his shoulder where his three markings hid beneath his top.

He tilted his head, the skin around one eye furrowing. "If you knew who I was, why didn't you say anything to me?"

"What difference would it have made? Even now?" Tomorrow was her appointment with the council to complete the public bonding to Blaine. Her lip trembled, and she bit the traitorous thing.

"It matters to me." He stroked a lock of her hair once again.

The sensation calmed her, yet made the agony all the more real, rawer. An urge to get away, to run and be free one last time overwhelmed her.

"Come with me." She gripped his hand, pulling him away from her workstation.

He didn't move, but held on to her hand, preventing her from leaving. "Where?"

"Please. I want to enjoy your company for as long as we can, even if it's just tonight." The implications of what she'd said raced through her mind, and she placed a hand over her mouth. As she was qithan, she shouldn't go, but the need to get away drove her onward. "I'm sorry. What I meant to say is that I want to go outside, enjoy the night, run free, be free." She swallowed. A small ribbon of doubt crept along her spine. "Will you go with me?"

The amber in his eyes darkened for a moment, and she'd never seen anything more alluring than the male standing next to her. A shiver ran over her shoulders. She wanted him more than she could express with words. It would take all her resolve to maintain propriety. Even so, he'd still break her heart—and further earn his reputation as a heartbreaker.

Without taking his gaze from her, he raised her hand to his mouth and gently kissed her fingers. "As you wish."

CHAPTER 17

"But the Portal Navigation Center is that way." Nicholai pointed down the long corridor. The sunstones lining the Keep's walls brightened in response, sensing his destination. Leonna pulled on his hand, the gentle nudge all that he needed to change his mind.

"I don't want anyone to see us leave." Her whispered words teased him. "Come, let's find one of the manual entrances. I'm sure we can get out and back before dawn."

As a warrior, he knew several of the manual entrances, the ones hidden from view of prying eyes, whether human or Gossum. "You know it's forbidden to leave through the manual entrances without alerting either the portal navigator or a council member."

She didn't speak, but the corner of her mouth lifted.

He shook his head, his own smile forming on his face. "I know of a way. Follow me."

To make this rash decision wasn't like him, his need to follow protocol screamed in his head, but she did this to him, she brought out his adventurous side. The tension in his chest lightened at the realization.

He led her down one of the side halls. They'd only passed a few others on the way here, and no one had paid them any particular attention. That was good. He'd rather not have to answer any inquiries. Where were they going? Why was he with her? What were they going to do? Those were questions he wasn't sure he could answer.

As they progressed further into the seldom used reaches of the Keep, the corridor narrowed. The sunstones lining the walls thinned to a single crystal spaced farther and farther apart. Dampness crept into the air. Still, he led her forward, his own desire to be with her driving him as much as her need to escape.

Their hands clasped together, he relished the softness and warmth of her skin. Memories of their time in the forest flooded his mind. His beast, sensing an opportunity for a repeat performance, fueled his energy, and he picked up his pace.

To take her again would be wrong. He shouldn't even be here with her now, but he couldn't stop, and if he was honest with himself, he didn't want to. His shoulder burned hot as his marking for duty faded. He felt the skin lighten, and his own guilt grew like a small knot in his gut.

The hair on the back of his neck rose. He stopped and Leonna bumped into him. Her firm breasts pressed into his back, and her hands landed on his waist.

Umpf. "Why'd you stop?"

He pressed his finger to his lips, and pointed behind them. She closed her mouth. He listened, straining to hear the slightest sound. Only their labored breaths echoed in the silent hallway. He thought he'd heard the slight squeak of boot against smooth stone. Was someone following them? He could've been wrong, but he didn't think so. They stood that way for several more seconds, watching, waiting. The stillness seemed to go on forever.

Leonna's warm body rubbed against him, encouraging his desire. He looked over his shoulder at her heated, inviting eyes. With a quickness born from his battle skills, he turned toward her and pinned her against the wall, caging her in his arms.

A delightful squeal escaped her lips. She wrapped her arms around his neck and giggled. Her hot breath tickled his neck, sending a shiver of delight down his back to his buttocks. He growled, letting her know she'd hit a nerve.

Cradling her head in his hand to protect her from the rough cave walls, he gave her a scorching kiss. She ran her fingernails over his scalp. The sensation both relaxed him and raised his craving for her. When he broke their connection, he stared into her eyes.

With his free hand, he trailed his fingertips down her throat to the thin chain of her necklace. He traced the golden string under the edge of her blouse to where the seashell rested in the "V" of her breasts. Her chest rose and fell in concert with her panted breaths. The carnal glimmer in her eyes just about did him in, but it was her breathless words that finished him off.

"Nicholai, please."

He picked her up, and she straddled her legs around his waist. Ravaging her with kisses, her soft mewls were all the response he needed. He growled. The sound echoed down the corridor. He broke their embrace, and ran his thumb along her plump bottom lip. "Not here, not in the tunnel."

She nodded, and he placed her back on her feet. They resumed their trek down the corridor. At each new turn, he expected to see a familiar sign. A small niggle of dread grew in his mind. Were they lost? He wouldn't admit this to her or himself.

They rounded a bend. He stilled in his tracks, holding his arm out to stop her. A giant chasm spread out before them in what used to be the passageway. "The Keep blocked this exit. Gossum must've found the entrance." The Keep looked after the inhabitants like a mother hen, and caused cave-ins to protect the residents.

Nicholai peered over the edge. Even with his preternatural vision, the sunstones didn't provide enough light to see the bottom.

"I think they went this way." From down the hall, the sound of his brother's voice sent a chill over Nicholai's skin.

They were in a no-win situation, trapped between an impassable fissure and his unrelenting brother. Nicholai wrapped his arm around Leonna and turned to face his sibling.

Feet pounding on the stone floor echoed down the hall as his brother and his posse approached. Tiernan rounded a bend and stopped. His two henchmen, Alden and Macion pulled up behind him. Tiernan glanced from Nicholai to Leonna.

"What are you doing down here?" Tiernan's eyes flashed with a hint of amusement, and his upper lip curled.

"Nothing that concerns you." Nicholai widened his stance and held his ground.

Tiernan and his cohorts crept closer.

"You ok there—Leonna? He hurt you?" Tiernan's gaze raked her body, and then he focused on her face.

Nicholai didn't like the lustful glint in Tiernan's eyes. *Protect. Mine.* Nicholai moved Leonna behind him, away from the other males. The ledge was dangerously close. A cold draft from the opening raised the hair on the back of his neck.

"I'm fine. Wh…what do you want?" Leonna wrapped her arm around Nicholai's waist, pressing against him. Her cheek rested against his shoulder.

"My, my, does my brother have a love in his life? That's a first." Tiernan chuckled. "Maybe we'll have some fun with her later, boys."

Nicholai's body shook with rage, and his vision blurred. *He's goading me.* A roar erupted from his throat. He wanted to rip the offending male in half, brother or not.

Leonna's grip tightened on his arm. "Please, don't. He's not worth the effort."

Nicholai fought the beast, taming him at her request. He focused on his brother, watching him like a hawk. "You followed me. Why?"

A flash caught Nicholai's attention.

In Tiernan's palm, the dagger he intended to give their father for his birthday glinted in the subdued light.

Tiernan's lip curled. "You made me look weak tonight, in front of the other males."

Nicholai took a step forward, balancing the distance between the two threats. Alden stood close by, his body tense, mouth set in a grim line. Macion hung back, brow furrowed.

Nicholai returned his gaze to his brother. "I think you did that all on your own."

Tiernan's face reddened. A low growl built in his chest.

Leonna gasped and took a step back.

Tiernan tensed and launched himself at Nicholai.

Grabbing the handle of his own dagger, Nicholai yanked the weapon from his belt.

The tip of Tiernan's blade swiped dangerously close to Nicholai's face.

He parried, blocking a blow from Tiernan's fist.

Leonna pushed against Nicholai, eager to get around him, her own anger evident in the tight lines in her face. She kicked Tiernan, landing a blow to his shin.

No. What was she doing? Nicholai's senses became hyper-sensitive to the world around him as his fear for her spiked. Caught up in his worry over his female, he lost focus for the briefest moment. That was all the time Tiernan needed.

Swoosh. Pain exploded in his shoulder.

His brother grunted and twisted the dagger.

The intensity of the pain radiated into Nicholai's head, threatening to fog his mind. He gripped the handle and pulled the dagger free. The tainted present clattered to the floor.

"Watch out!" Leonna's voice broke through the fog in his mind just in time.

Nicholai flipped his own dagger to his uninjured hand and thrust out, toward his assailant. The tip connected with his brother's face. A thin, red line of blood formed along his cheek.

"Help me, you fools." Tiernan's voice, full of malice echoed down the corridor.

"*Craya.* No way." Alden ran.

Nicholai caught a glimpse of Macion. The male held back, watching. His furrowed brows and taut face belayed his confusion.

Leonna edged closer to the ledge, away from the males.

Nicholai stilled, fear gripping his heart like a vise.

Smack. His head whipped to the side, and his vision blurred. He faltered from the agony.

Using the shift in momentum, Tiernan rushed at Nicholai, sending him into Leonna.

Leonna's scream echoed off the walls as she fell into the crevasse.

Noooooooooo. He glanced over the edge.

She was gone.

Adrenaline fueled by hatred raced through Nicholai's body. In a rage, he picked up his brother, and body-slammed him to the ground. He held the knife to Tiernan's neck. *He's my brother.* The familial bond was the only reason the insolent male wasn't dead.

The urge to push the blade into Tiernan's throat made Nicholai's fingers twitch, nicking the skin. A drop of blood pooled at the blade's tip before tracing a line along his brother's throat and dripping to the ground.

Tiernan's chest heaved from his quick breaths. He parted his lips and hissed, spittle flying from his mouth. "I hate you."

Nicholai blinked. Rage clouded his mind. His hand gripped the dagger so hard his hand shook.

"You were always father's favorite." Tiernan pulled his arm from under his back, the dropped dagger in his palm.

He slashed Nicholai's forearm, the deep cut sending a sharp pain into his hand. His favorite weapon fell from his grasp, slid over Tiernan's shoulder, and clattered on the stone floor.

Nicholai grabbed his brother's wrist, and the two fought for the fated dagger. Wrestling like dogs, they came close to the edge of the crevasse.

Tiernan rolled one too many times, coming to a stop with his legs dangling over the edge. He stilled then his body relaxed against Nicholai.

With heavy breaths, Nicholai looked at his brother. The tip of the dagger protruded from Tiernan's chest.

What have I done?

His brother's body began decomposing, his fingers and arms

turning to sand. The gilded dagger lay nearby, and Nicholai kicked the offending weapon over the side.

The edge of the crevasse brought back the memory of his love. A fear so great squeezed his chest, making it difficult to breath.

"Leonna." Nicholai kneeled and peered over the cliff. Where was she? Blackness enveloped the space like the vastness of the universe without any stars.

The sound of quick footsteps approaching made him turn.

Macion raised his hands. "I want to help. I'm not here to fight you —Prince."

Nicholai turned to face the blackness. His greatest fear manifested itself in his gut. He'd lost Leonna, his love. He was responsible for her death. A wave of dizziness engulfed him. He couldn't move. Memories of Rand and his demise at the hands of the Gossum flooded his mind.

Nicholai's heavy breaths were the only sound in the still air.

Macion placed his hand on Nicholai's shoulder. "Step away from the edge. It's not safe."

Nicholai's body was as immovable as stone. A heavy weight descended on his shoulders, pinning him there like nothing else could. His marking for courage faded. The thin line burned as the circle disappeared under his skin. He truly was a failure.

CHAPTER 18

*N*icholai couldn't breathe. His mind fogged. Kneeling at the edge of the crevasse, he stared into the empty space. *Leonna—she's gone.*

"Nick, move back, away from the edge." Macion placed his hand under Nicholai's arm and pulled. "Let me help you."

Riveted to the floor as if he were made of stone, Nicholai remained frozen. *Leonna—she's gone.*

"I'm going to get help. Be right back." Macion's footsteps receded.

The quiet enveloped Nicholai. He didn't know how long he knelt there on the edge, his only focus on the loss of his love. *I never told her how much she meant to me.* Regret dug a hole in his heart, picking at the organ until anguish was all he felt. He closed his eyes and accepted the pain. *Leonna—she's gone.*

The Keep rumbled. Tiny bits of rock and dirt rained down on Nicholai's head.

A soft whimper pierced through the fog in his brain. He tensed and opened his eyes.

The low moan grew louder.

Adrenaline surged through his veins. He jumped to his feet and peered over the edge. Blackness greeted him, along with the slight scent of honey. "Leonna!"

A small avalanche fell from inside the crevasse. Rocks pinged against the walls, but there was no indication they ever hit bottom.

"Ow. Ow."

"Leonna. Don't move."

"Ni...Nicholai? Where am—"

Her panicked cry echoed from the chasm. "Nicholai, the ledge, it's giving way."

Fear clawed at his soul. A coldness he'd never experienced before chilled him. His feet wouldn't move. She'd die unless he helped her.

The few sunstones lining the walls brightened to a radiant glow. Her eyes reflected the light, and the outline of her form became visible. She lay on a small ledge about ten feet down.

She looked up at him. "Nicholai...help me. I believe in you."

His heart expanded. The ice in his veins melted, just a tad. His breath caught in his throat as a tendril of hope weaseled its way into his soul.

"Leonna." His word was but a whisper, and a step in the right direction.

She leaned against the chasm wall and raised herself to her feet. A portion of the ledge she'd been laying on a few seconds ago broke off and fell into the void below. Her eyes tinged with fear, but as her gaze locked with his, her features softened. Confidence and faith replaced her fright. "Nicholai, you're not that young newb anymore, you're different. Remember, you saved me from that male on Betram night. Help me now, I know you can."

Her trust and certainty in his ability to save her rocked him to the core. Belief in himself grew, like a tiny sprout. His love for her nurtured the little shoot, and confidence blossomed in his soul. His marking for courage pulsed to life.

Breaking free from his immobility, his body flexed, blood flowing through his veins. He lay flat on the ground, his arms and shoulders leaning over the edge. As he reached for her, a drop of blood traced down his arm and dripped from his fingertip. Fear threatened to take over his mind, but he focused on the faith in her eyes.

She stood on her tip-toes. Both of them stretched their fingers, but they were a foot too short.

Another shower of rocks plunged from the narrow ledge, forcing her to hug the rocks protruding from the side.

She still believed, he could see it in the depths of her eyes.

With a conviction born of his love for her, he made a dangerous decision. "Hang on. I'm going to change."

To loosen the beast inside the Keep was forbidden. Hard to control even on the battlefield, Stiyaha were known to wreak havoc if not tightly restrained. For him to even consider breaking the rules indicated just how much he'd changed. He'd take this chance for her and suffer the consequences if he failed.

She nodded once and hugged the wall.

He stepped away from the ledge and opened his mind. The synapses fired, connecting man to beast. His bones and muscles crackled and popped. He grew to his full nine feet, his clothing disappearing beneath the fur.

Fueled by the freedom, the beast roared at the top of his lungs. His beast understood the threat to his female, and the frustration and fear were just more fuel, more energy to use in the fight. The problem—this wasn't the kind of fight the beast could handle. Nicholai calmed himself, soothing the beast, impressing the need to protect Leonna.

Together as one with his beast, he lay on the surface of the cold stone floor. As he leaned over the edge, his upper body and arms stretched farther than before.

She reached up to meet him. Love, respect, and trust all radiated from her expression. Their fingers entwined, and he gripped her wrists. He scooted back, inch by inch, pulling her upward.

The ledge gave way, the final rocks falling into the chasm. They pinged off the edge until they could no longer be heard.

Running feet echoed down the hallway, registering in the back of his mind. He couldn't worry about that threat right now. The need to save his female burned under his skin.

She hung from his grip. The slick blood on his fingers made her slip.

His heart caught in his throat. *Nooooo.*

With the strength born into his beast, he pulled her over the edge and enfolded her in his arms. She wrapped herself around him, sitting in his lap. His beast huffed, breathing in her unique scent, the one he'd memorized during Betram. All was right in the world, at least in that moment.

"You...You saved her." Macion whispered.

"He's in beast form. Stay back." A male's voice permeated Nicholai's mind.

A third male chimed in. "He doesn't appear to be a threat. He's holding her in his lap."

"Nicholai, I'm okay. Let me go." Leonna's words broke through the beast's control.

As much as he didn't want to release her, he'd do as she requested. She stood, and the loss of her warmth made his chest constrict.

The males in the room tensed and they reached for their swords.

"No, don't." She held out her hands.

Nicholai rose to his feet and glared at the males. His muscles quivered as anger rippled over his skin. His beast wanted a good fight and these males seemed up for the challenge.

Leonna placed her hand on his arm. "Nicholai." Like a bird's wings, his name on her lips fluttered over his psyche, calming him.

These males weren't a threat. In the back of his mind, his rational brain knew this. He pulled on the strings connecting to his beast, encouraging his alter ego to go back to sleep. The beast retreated, and he changed back into his human physique. Pants, shirt, and boots all reformed as if he'd never taken them off.

"You saved me." Leonna's gaze locked onto his.

"No, you saved me. You believed in me and helped me overcome my fear." He clasped her hand, the one with only the index finger, and brought it to his lips for a gentle kiss.

"What of Tiernan?" Macion crept toward the edge, but wouldn't get too close. A small mound of sand was all that remained of Nicholai's brother.

Nicholai shook his head. "Gone." A pang of regret hit him in the gut.

"It's not your fault." Leonna placed her hand on his chest.

"He attacked. You defended yourself." Macion pointed to the other two males. "Be my witness, I confess this to be the truth. Prince Nicholai is innocent in the death of his brother."

Both males bowed, acknowledging Macion's declaration.

Blood dripped onto the stone floor. Aware of the gash in his arm, Nicholai's pain reared to life once again. He gritted his teeth, unwilling to show his weakness in front of the males.

"You should get that checked out." Macion pointed to his wound. "We'll tell the council and your father what happened."

"No. I'll tell my father." His circle for duty pulsed. An easy conversation? No, but this was something he must do.

"As you wish." Macion nodded. He and the other two males exited the room, leaving Nicholai alone with Leonna.

A smile crossed Leonna's face, but then she stilled. The smile faltered.

Dread raced along his nerves. "What is it?"

"I have to get back. I'll meet up with you later. I promise." She leaned against him and pecked him on the lips.

He pulled her to him, deepening the kiss, telling her without words just what she meant to him. When they finally parted, their combined breaths were loud in the empty corridor.

"I'm going to hold you to that promise." He kissed her once more then they raced down the hallway.

CHAPTER 19

*L*eonna stood outside Blaine's door. The muscles in her back and shoulders tightened. She pursed her lips, and raised her fist. A muffled moan from the other side made her halt, her knuckles mere inches from the old wooden door.

She glanced down the corridor. An elderly couple stopped at the entrance to one of the other rooms in the passageway. The female swayed on her feet. The male cradled her elbow in his hand, steadying her. Their white hair and wrinkled skin revealed their advanced age. Two black bonding bands surrounded his neck. His tender care made Leonna's chest constrict.

She couldn't imagine Blaine, her qithan, ever treating her with such affection. That's why she was here—to put an end to this sham. All her life she'd bent to others' demands, like a blade of grass in the wind. She'd never made a decision for herself. Her life had been prescribed, dictated to her from the day she was born. The knuckles in her fist cracked from her fury.

She faced Blaine's door once again. Muffled voices filtered through the cracks. She placed her hand against the rough grain and leaned forward. The door opened.

Her instincts went on high alert. Blood pounded in her ears. Voices came from the far corner of the room.

"Blaine?" she whispered.

No response. She pushed on the door. *Creak.*

"What the— Who's there?" Blaine's voice was tight, strained.

Rustling sheets and feet padding along the floor carried across the room.

Leonna crossed the threshold and peered around the edge of the door. She gaped at Blaine who stood naked in front of her, a sheet haphazardly wrapped around the front of his torso, his erection tenting the fabric. Behind him, on the bed, was another male. His eyes widened when he caught her gaze. He grabbed the pillow from behind his head and placed the cushion over his crotch.

Leonna clamped her hand over her mouth. She couldn't process what her eyes showed her. Although same-sex coupling wasn't forbidden, she didn't expect this from her qithan.

"What are you doing here?" Blaine's face contorted into a mask of horror.

"I could ask the same of you." She spit the words out, but deep inside the weight on her chest lightened. He'd just made this conversation a whole lot easier.

The gold qithan bracelet burned against her skin. She unclasped the heavy chain and threw the symbol of his promise at his feet. Turning on her heel, she headed for the door.

"Leonna…wait. I can explain—"

She didn't slow down and slammed the door in her wake.

Whoosh. The double doors opened, creating a soft breeze that caressed Nicholai's cheek. How many times had he entered the throne room? More than he cared to count. The smell of age and antiquity mixed with his mother's scent of lavender. The strange blend didn't ease his anxiety, not with the news he brought. At the end of the short entryway, his father sat on his throne, his mother on the cushioned dais at his side. Her hand rested in the crook of his arm.

She caught Nicholai's gaze. The lines around her eyes creased as she smiled.

His chest constricted.

Councilman Gareth bowed low before the king, his cape wrapping around his shoulders like a bat's wings. "Thank you, Your Majesty, I shall attend to your request immediately." The male rose and as he turned, his cape flared out behind him. His quick strides brought him close to Nicholai, and he gave him a quick nod in greeting. "Prince."

Nicholai nodded in return. As Gareth left, Kit closed the door behind him, leaving Nicholai in the room with his parents. He tried to step forward, but his feet wouldn't move. Heavy with the news of Tiernan's death, he didn't want to break his mother's heart, but he had no choice. They needed to know.

"Nicholai, what is it? You're pale, and your arm—" His mother rose from her perch, her fingers outstretched, pointing at his injury.

Her worry loosened his muscles. He walked to her side and clasped her hands. "I'm fine mother, but I bring sad news." He glanced at his father.

"What is this news?" King Monroe sat forward in his chair, his elbow resting on his knee. His gaze pierced into Nicholai's soul.

"Tiernan...he's dead." A rush of adrenaline pooled in Nicholai's stomach.

King Monroe stood, his body rigid. His brow furrowed, as if he couldn't believe the words. "W...What? How?"

On the trek back through the Keep, this was the question he'd thought about over and over again. His marking for courage and conviction drove him forward. He inhaled a large breath and spoke the truth. "I killed him."

His father visibly flinched, and his gaze roamed Nicholai's face.

A small hitch escaped his mother's lips. Her dais creaked as she sat down.

Nicholai worked hard to control his breathing. The shocked look in his father's eyes just about broke him. Silence filled the room, except for the pounding of his own heart.

Monroe's eyes narrowed. "What did you do?"

Nicholai knew they'd blame him. He was bad luck to anyone that got too close. "It matters not. I wanted to be the one to tell you, before you heard from someone else."

His father shook his head, the lines in his face more pronounced, deeper. He'd aged many years in the past few minutes. "Leave us. I need time alone…to process this." He waved his hand in the air.

Nicholai glanced at his mother. She covered her eyes with one hand. A tear dripped off the end of her finger and landed on her dress. The wetness left a dark spot, one that matched the ache in his chest.

With a deep heaviness in his heart, he left his parents to mourn the loss of their son. His brain couldn't handle the overload, and he let his feet lead him. Where he went, he cared not.

CHAPTER 20

a s Leonna approached her family's residence, she slowed her pace. The walls of the Keep seemed to bear down on her. The weight of the qithan had been like a collar around her throat, the leash attached to her father's hand. No more. She wouldn't let her father dictate to her which male she bonded to. An image of Nicholai crossed her mind, his intense gaze penetrating into her heart. Her hand clenched into a fist. *I can't have him.*

Nicholai was a member of the royal family, part of the elite inner circle. As a common merchant, she couldn't be a part of that. Besides, despite his kisses, the ones that told her that he cared, he'd made no mention of his feelings for her.

The relief that had coursed through her veins disappeared, replaced with regret. She took a breath, but couldn't seem to fill her lungs with air. Although she was no longer qithan, she still had her responsibility to her family—the honey cart. Her chest clenched tighter.

She rounded a corner and a Jixie bumped into her. The small female landed on her behind, green beans falling out of the basket she carried and scattering across the floor. The look on her face was priceless, her mouth contorted into an 'oh,' her eyes wide.

"I'm so sorry." Leonna helped the little Jixie to her feet.

The young female straightened her dress, mud stains streaking the once vibrant yellow a gritty brown color. " 'Twas my fault, m'lady, not yourns." She didn't make eye contact, but proceeded to pick up the beans.

Leonna assisted, grabbing a handful of the vegetables that had landed in the crack between the wall and the floor. The waxy beans smelled fresh, like the garden. She held out her hand, the beans dangling over the edge of her palm. "These are dirty. Will you be in trouble?"

The Jixie finally met Leonna's gaze. Her deep, green eyes contrasted with her bright red hair. The difference was striking. "Doesn't matter. 'Twas my fault. M' mind wanders and…" Shrugging, she corralled the last of the stray pods. She gave one last glance at Leonna before sprinting down the hallway. Even for a Jixie, her little feet moved fast.

She reminds me of myself. A new sense of understanding made her knees shake. The evening's events raced through her mind—Nicholai discovering her necklace, their kiss, her desire to escape the Keep and run free, the chasm, the fall, Nicholai's rescue. Dizziness made her vision blur. She placed her hands against the rough stone of the corridor walls and closed her eyes. *My impulsiveness—causes trouble for myself and others. I can't be that way anymore.*

The responsibility to her family and their reliance on her was a burden, one she'd harbored for a long time. Her destiny was the honey business, her role in the Keep, and she wouldn't let her father down.

Her heart beat steady and strong as she accepted her commitment. As she walked the few remaining feet to her family's quarters, she steeled herself. The discussion with Papa wouldn't be easy. He'd be hard to convince that she'd changed.

She gripped the doorknob and entered her home. The room contained the same table with the flower vase, the rack filled with leftover sample jars of honey, and the pictures of her and Corbin that she'd painted, but her home seemed different. Somehow, she felt confined, restricted.

"Oh, you're home. Hello, hon." Maman emerged from her parents' bedroom. She smiled as if nothing had changed.

"Is...is Papa here?" A burning need to see him right away made her edgy.

"Did I hear my name?" Her father limped into the room. His gait seemed more pronounced, as if he were in pain.

"Papa, are you ok?" Leonna held her breath.

"Just a bit tired, that's all." His smile was the one she remembered from her childhood, but she didn't need his approval, not anymore.

She gripped his hand, squeezing his fingers. "I have something to tell you, something important."

He gazed into her eyes. "Do tell."

"I made a decision...a couple of decisions." She swallowed. This was harder than she'd anticipated.

He didn't speak, but cocked an eyebrow.

She pulled on her courage and raised her chin. "I won't bond to Blaine. I don't love him, and he's a cheat."

Her father's eyebrows furrowed, and he dropped his hands, breaking their connection. "Really?" He rubbed his face and let out a loud exhale.

Before he could say anything more, she dove in. "I can handle the honey cart on my own. I won't be late, I'll make sure all the stones are counted at the end of the day, I'll stay late to clean up, I'll—"

Her father held up his hand.

She bit her lip.

"Tell her, Riordan." Leonna's mother stood at the counter, combining the honey samples into a larger jar. Her smile was infectious, and she winked at Leonna.

Leonna's stomach fluttered, as if birds had found their way in. "What's going on?"

"Your timing is uncanny." He chuckled. "When you are finally ready to take ownership of the honey cart, we no longer need you to."

"What?" She blinked. Her mind couldn't process what he'd just said.

"Corbin!" he bellowed.

Her brother emerged from his bedroom, and he wasn't alone. On his arm was a young female with short blond hair and striking blue eyes. One look at her brother's throat answered all her questions. Two black bands circled his neck. He'd bonded to this female.

Corbin grinned. "Leonna, this is Em, my mate."

Em gripped Leonna's hand with warm, strong fingers. "I'm so happy to meet you. I've heard nothing but good things about you."

Leonna couldn't help the smile that formed on her lips. By the sparkle in her brother's eyes, this female had stolen his heart. Leonna embraced her new sister, thankful for the opportunity to get to know her. "I'm so happy for the both of you. How—"

"Betram. Oh, and I quit the training program." Corbin wrapped his arm around his new mate's shoulder. "We're going to run the honey cart together." His smile was all Leonna needed to see to understand his happiness.

"That means you can paint, if you want to." Her father's voice was low, comforting. "I put too much pressure on you. I should've thought more about your feelings. I'm sorry, daughter mine."

Leonna rushed into her father's arms. "Thank you, Papa."

As he petted her hair, her heart expanded.

He pulled away and cradled her head in his hands. "Now, tell me about Blaine."

She stilled and looked at the ground. What could she say? No good could come from telling him what she'd seen. Instead, she settled for a half-truth. "He found someone else."

"I'm sorry, daughter. Perhaps I can find someone for you."

"No! Don't!" She held his gaze. There was only one male she wanted. An urge to see Nicholai built in her soul. She wanted to bolt to him, tell him she loved him. *And that's what gets me in trouble, my compulsiveness.* Instead, she lifted her chin and held her ground. "I can find my own mate."

He nodded, a sly smile lifting at the corner of his mouth. "My grown-up daughter, as you wish."

Reflexively, she gripped the seashell on the end of her chain. The shell was warm from resting against the skin on her chest. She wasn't sure she believed in the old ritual. At the time, she hadn't known what she'd wanted, but she did now.

"Lea, I wasn't wrong." Maman pointed at Leonna's closed fist. "The sun infused the shell with good luck. You'll see."

Against Leonna's will, she evoked an image of Nicholai. If only her mother were right.

CHAPTER 21

$\mathcal{B}$efore Nicholai knew it, he stood outside the door to the infirmary. Of course, he'd come here. Maybe a discussion with Gaetan would help ease his spirit. He knocked.

"Door's open."

Nicholai entered the room, and the smell of disinfectant was a familiar, yet calming salve. Gaetan leaned against the counter. His shoulders flexed as he ground medicinal herbs in a stone bowl. He glanced at Nicholai then resumed his work.

Nicholai wasn't sure what to say. He'd come here, but now, he questioned why. His teeth ground together so hard a tic started in his jaw.

"What's on your mind? Your brother?" Gaetan continued to press the wooden grinder against the leaves. The scraping sound echoed around the room.

"You already know about my brother?"

Gaetan stopped his work and gave Nicholai a pointed stare. "Word travels fast along the stones, as you know."

"I killed him." The confession came out in a rush of words. Funny, admitting it didn't make Nicholai feel any better.

Gaetan raised an eyebrow. "In self-defense, I hear. But your brother isn't what brings you here, is it?"

Nicholai chuckled, eased a bit by Gaetan's candor. "You know me so well. I can't hide anything from you."

The skin on Gaetan's forehead creased, and his eyes brightened. "From your reactions the past few days, I suspect you found a female at the Betram ritual."

"Was it that obvious?"

"To me, yes. What concerns you?"

"The tradition to select a female from the elite class as a mate—how firm is that?" He tensed, waiting for Gaetan's answer.

Gaetan blinked, but maintained his composure. "Kings for countless millennia have selected their mates from the eligible elite females. I take it your female in question isn't one of them."

He held Gaetan's gaze, sure in his choice. "No, she's merchant class, but that matters not to me."

Gaetan nodded, but the hint of a smile crossed his face. "Traditions, like rules, were meant to be broken."

Nicholai's chest constricted, hope welling inside. "Until the past few hours, I hadn't broken a rule since—"

Gaetan raised a hand. "Maybe a little rule breaking is what you need."

"Perhaps you're right." Nicholai couldn't stop the smile that pulled at his lip.

Gaetan returned to his work, the grinder scraping against the bowl once again. "I can't wait to meet her."

"At the moment, she's qithan to another male. I pray I'm not too late." Nicholai bolted for the door, intent on getting his answer.

Leonna walked past the other artists hard at work on their paintings. The sound of brushes swishing and chairs creaking made her smile. At this point, anything could make her smile now. She was free, as free as a bird. Embracing her new life, her heart swelled. A small niggle started in her chest, and she felt restless. What of Nicholai? He'd headed straight to the throne room to tell his parents the news of his brother.

As she arrived at her stand, Wren raced over to her and gripped her hands. "Leonna, good to see you again."

She blinked and furrowed her brow. "Um, good to see you, too."

He glanced around at the other artists and patrons that filled the large cavern.

A warning bell rang in her mind. She tensed. "What's going on?"

He looked behind him, toward her canvas. "Your painting of Prince Nicholai…" He faced her and bit his lip.

"What about it?" She peered around him. A sheet hung over her painting, obscuring the picture from view. A sour taste rose in the back of her throat.

He stepped aside. "I concealed the canvas so no one would see."

She bolted toward her work and ripped off the covering. She stilled. Goosebumps rose along her arms. A large gash ran the length of the painting, from one corner to the other. The damage was irreparable.

"No. No. Who would do this?" She fisted her hands. Her body shook, as a rage built within her, one fueled by her love for Nicholai.

"I…I know who did this. I saw it happen," Wren whispered.

She spoke through gritted teeth. "Who?"

He glanced around again, but no one paid any attention to them. "Prince Tiernan. I left and forgot to put my favorite brush in the cleaning solution. When I came back it was late, no one else was here, or so I thought. I saw him cut the painting. I hid in another stall until he left."

She was sure Tiernan did this with the dagger he intended to give to his father. Placing her hand on Wren's shoulder, she gave him a reassuring smile. "Thank you for telling me."

He relaxed and a nervous laugh rose from his chest. "Sure. I'm sorry I didn't stop him."

"You were smart to stay clear of Tiernan. It doesn't matter now, anyway. He's dead."

"Dead? How?" Wren raised his eyebrows.

The smell of cloves and rain filtered into Leonna's senses, calming her, warming her on the inside. *Nicholai.*

Nicholai stared hard at Wren. He looked ravaged, beaten from the inside out.

Wren tensed and turned in a slow circle. "Uh, Leonna, I gotta go. I'll talk to you later." With that, he walked away at a clipped pace, getting lost among the other artists and patrons.

"Nicholai, what's wrong?" Leonna ran her hand up his arm, and she touched the fresh scab that covered his injury. "You still haven't taken care of this?"

"It's too late now. The gash is healing on its own. Guess I'll get a pretty scar." He moved a stray strand of hair from her cheek. His gaze roamed her face, a tender gleam in his eyes, his own private medication.

"I'm glad you're here." She smiled and his shoulders visibly relaxed.

"Me, too." A slow smile curved at the corner of his mouth, and an overwhelming urge to kiss those delectable lips pulled her closer to him.

He wrapped his fingers in her hair, cradling her head in his hand. Ultra-sensitive to his touch, her body reacted to his ministrations, sending a rush of warmth between her legs. His pupils dilated, and his gaze focused on her lips. She licked them in invitation, daring him to kiss her.

He complied. His warm, wet mouth pressed against hers, bruising her lips with the force of his passion. He pulled her to him, and his erection pressed against her abdomen, flaring her desire. She moaned, memories of their coupling on Betram night and the heady endorphins rushing through her body. She dug her nails into his biceps and, the realization hit her—this is what she really wanted—him.

She threaded her fingers into his hair, the sensation teasing the raw nerves in her fingertips. His desire fueled hers, and she bit him on the lip. He growled, the sound possessive and demanding. She loved his reaction, all male, all for her.

He finally let her go so they could catch their breath. His chest heaved from his exertion, and she panted right along with him. He traced a finger from her forehead, pausing long enough to caress her cheek before cradling her chin. His eyes followed his movement, the look of devotion so intense, she felt cherished, loved by this strong, powerful male.

He continued his journey down her arm. When he reached her wrist, he stilled. His gaze shot to hers. His eyes shifted back and forth, and his brow furrowed. "Where's your bracelet?"

A warmth built in her chest and radiated into her smile. "I gave the dreaded jewelry back. I'm no longer qithan."

He studied her, his eyes intense. A mischievous smile lifted the corner of his mouth. "That's the best news I've heard all day. Would you like to be?"

She inhaled. Now it was her turn to examine him. His smile, the glint in his eye, and if she didn't know better, she'd think he'd just asked her—

He wrapped his fingers around hers and brought them to his lips. "Well?"

"I don't know what to say."

"Whatever you'd like. I'd tell you I care not, but that would be a lie." He brushed his mouth against the back of her hand, giving her a gentle kiss. When he spoke, his voice deepened. "Leonna, I…love you. Will you become *my* qithan?"

Her throat constricted, and she held her breath for several seconds. With a dry swallow, she spit the words out in a rush. "But I'm not one of the elite…I'm a merchant."

Amber flashed through his blue eyes, and he shook his head. "That's a tradition, not a requirement, and it's one tradition I intend to break."

She pulled on her neck chain and held the small seashell. Maman was right, the charm was good luck. A happiness she'd never known before warmed her soul. "Yes, Nicholai…I'll become your qithan."

He kissed her again. She'd finally made a decision all on her own— the right one.

CHAPTER 22

*T*he Grand Hall buzzed with activity as Stiyaha and Jixies alike prepared for the king's birthday celebration. Baskets of apples, pears, and assorted berries lined the tables along the wall. A Jixie wearing an apron, stained brown from use, carried a basket full of sweetbreads. She placed them next to the whipped cream and pies. The smell of the baked goods filled the air. Nicholai's stomach rumble.

Leaning against a stack of chairs in the corner of the room, he watched in amazement and stayed out of the way. Leonna snuggled next to him. Her body rubbed against his, lighting a fire under his skin. He still wasn't used to the warmth that spread in his chest when he looked at her. He'd cherish her for the rest of his life.

"I've never seen preparation such as this." She glanced at the ceiling, where a couple of female Stiyahas stood on ladders, hanging ribbons from a center ring. The gentle arch of the material flared at the base and hooked into hoops at the corners of the room.

He pulled her closer, enjoying her contact. Even with her here, he had difficulty swallowing. The lump in the back of his throat wouldn't go down. His parents, the honored guests, would arrive soon. How would his father would react to seeing him here? He let out a sigh and forced himself not to dwell on something he had no control over.

The ladders came down and two warriors carried them out of the room.

"Nicholai?" Leonna's scrunched forehead and wide eyes portrayed her worry.

She knew something bothered him.

"What is it? Tell me."

"The king!" Audible gasps and frantic footsteps filled the air.

"Be quiet. Gather round, hurry!" someone shouted.

The packed chamber had a capacity of three hundred. There was easily twice the number jammed in the large space. Others crowded next to Nicholai and Leonna. All he could do was pull her even closer to make room.

A cheer erupted from the crowd closest to the entrance. "Hail, King Monroe!"

Someone in the crowd started the birthday song. Voices raised in unison to sing.

Birthday come, birthday go

Nicholai joined in, his voice strained.

A year, a decade, a century passes

Despite the crowd of well-wishers gathered around him, he caught his father's gaze.

Birthday come, birthday go

The old male nodded, a gleam of acceptance in his eyes.

May you return for another, not your last

The crowd erupted into cheers once again.

Nicholai's muscles relaxed, tension draining from his limbs. His father wouldn't hold his brother's death against him. He wanted to shout his happiness from the top of his lungs. Leonna squeezed his hand. He rubbed his chin on the top of her head and kissed her hair.

For those lucky enough to be selected via lottery to attend today's celebration, the party that ensued was one that would be remembered and talked about for decades.

As his father and mother made their way through the crowd, Nicholai had second thoughts. Maybe his father hadn't forgiven him.

"Nicholai. Stop fretting." Leonna rubbed her hand down his arm, soothing him with her touch.

An encouraging smile graced her plump lips. He bent down, capturing them. Blood rushed through his veins, calming him and exciting him at the same time. He clasped her hands in his and kissed her fingers, all seven of them.

She looked over his shoulder and raised her chin, wanting him to take notice. He turned just in time to see his father, breaking through the crowd.

Nicholai kept Leonna behind him in a protective gesture. He didn't want her involved if his father intended to berate him in public.

"Nicholai?" His name sounded odd coming from his father's lips, as if the old male were unsure who he was. With a distant gaze, he seemed to lose focus, but then he blinked and the brightness returned to his eyes. "Nicholai!"

"Well wishes to you on your one-thousandth birthday." Nicholai gave a short bow in respect, but didn't break eye contact.

His father didn't speak, but the lines around his eyes softened. "My son." He pulled Nicholai into a strong hug, pounding his back with his fists.

Nicholai's heart raced and his breath caught in his throat. "Father—?"

The elder male pulled away, his eyes moist with unshed tears. "Macion stopped by—why didn't you tell me Tiernan attacked you?"

Nicholai blinked. "It matters no—"

The king raised his hand. "Don't say it!" He pursed his lips. "It matters *a lot.*"

Nicholai shook his head. "Who started the fight doesn't change the fact that I killed him."

"Self-defense." His father rubbed his eyes and huffed. When he opened them, an intensity Nicholai rarely saw radiated from their depths. "Your brother will go back to Lemuria, but he won't receive a warrior's rite. He doesn't deserve one."

Nicholai exhaled, but held his tongue. As king, his father had every right to prohibit the death ceremony, their most sacred ritual.

The old male wiped his face and peered at Nicholai. "Macion mentioned that you overcame your fear, you saved someone you care about."

Leonna moved to Nicholai's side. "He saved me."

His mother raised an eyebrow. "And who is this young female?"

In the intensity of the moment with his father, he'd forgotten about Leonna. His neck and ears heated at his thoughtlessness. He stood tall as a sense of pride filled him. "This is Leonna, my qithan. She's a painter."

His mother inhaled a quick breath and glanced between him and Leonna. "The old tradition—" She stopped and shook her head. "Well, as the future king, you have the right to do as you please. Just know, not everyone will accept your decision, but given enough time, even the stubborn ones will come around." A smile broke out on her face, turning her cheeks pink. "Oh...I'm so happy for the two of you." She clasped Leonna's hands then pulled her into an embrace.

"Now, that's a decision a king would make." King Monroe clapped his hand on Nicholai's shoulder. "I couldn't have asked for a better birthday present."

Nicholai smiled, thankful that he'd pleased his finicky father. "She painted a picture of me for you as your gift, but the portrait was ruined—"

Shhhh. King Monroe held his finger to his lips. He leaned in and whispered loudly to Leonna. "Paint me a family portrait, when you have a young one. The picture shall be my gift to my grandchild."

Leonna's cheeks reddened, but she handled herself with aplomb. "Of course, I shall be delighted."

"Where's her qithan bracelet?" Queen Pia glanced at Nicholai.

He grimaced. "I haven't had time to give one to her, yet."

His father laughed. "There'll be plenty of time to celebrate. It's not every day that a future king is qithan."

Nicholai stilled and stared at his father. To mention his future role was an indication that he'd truly forgiven him. "Thank you, Father."

He pulled Leonna into his arms, smelling her sweet honey scent. She'd taught him to open up and trust in himself. She'd made him whole. He'd love her until the day he died. Lifting her chin, he gave her a tender kiss. Passion for her burned in his soul. A young? He couldn't wait to get started.

EPILOGUE

SEVERAL YEARS LATER...

*L*eonna picked up her favorite paintbrush and studied the tip. The fine hairs wouldn't last much longer. She sighed. Although she'd miss this one, she needed to find a different brush, soon. Dipping the end into the brown pigment, she glanced at her current work, a portrait—one she'd promised a king several years ago.

The picture would take time. She wouldn't rush to complete such an important task. The smell of the oil mixed with Nicholai's scent and she closed her eyes, relishing the moment. She loved her caring, gentle mate. Bonding to him was the best decision she'd ever made. During the physical bonding they'd been fortunate—he'd received two black bonding bands around his throat, signifying a good, happy relationship.

A child's laughter brought her out of her musing. *Noeh.* She glanced at her son. Even as a child, he had his father's build, and the angle of his nose and the shape of his ears were the spitting image of his sire. His short blond hair and the contour of his blue eyes came from her. She took in a breath, and her lungs expanded so much, her chest ached. Noeh sat across from Nicholai at a small wooden table whose grain had pockmarks, evidence of its constant use.

The worn furniture was in stark contrast to the opulence of the fine furnishings in their private chamber. In the corner was a large four-poster bed with a blue and green comforter, the colors of the royal family. Her dresser, filled with assorted bottles and grooming supplies, hugged one wall while Nicholai's bureau sat against the other. Much taller than hers, his dresser was bare, except for his brush. A small antechamber led off to Noeh's portion of the residence, and a hallway connected to the royal bath.

Her paintings lined the walls—many, many paintings. Her career as an artist took off after she'd created the picture of Nicholai, despite its ruination. How much of that was due to her status as future queen, she wasn't sure. As Nicholai often said, 'It matters not.' She chuckled to herself.

"How do you always manage to get the good rolls?" Nicholai pursed his lips, but the corner of his mouth crept into a grin. He looked at his son, and his eyes flecked with gold.

Leonna dipped her brush into the amber pigment, adding the touch to the painting.

Noeh laughed. "You should try harder." He picked up a handful of sunstones and tossed them across the table. His brow bunched in concentration while he studied the pattern the crystals created.

A warmth radiated from her soul. As she brushed the paint onto the canvas, she moved to her own rhythm, adding fine details.

Noeh glanced at his father and sniggered. He picked up a stone and moved it to another spot on the table. The alignment of the stones was the key to winning the game.

"Really? Un-uh. I've got you now." A smile spread across Nicholai's face, and he picked up another stone. He held it in mid-air. His smile faltered. "Wait. Um…" He bit his lip then shot a glance at Noeh. "Sneaky, sneaky…"

Noeh's infectious laugh echoed around the chamber.

Nicholai placed the stone back on the table. "Well...shoot. You got me."

"Yeah! I won!" Noeh held up an orange sunstone, like the crystal was the best victory ever.

Leonna captured the moment, both in her heart and on her canvas. As she examined her work, she touched the chain around her throat. She'd painted herself into the scene, along with her necklace—the one that had brought them together.

She glanced at Nicholai, and her heart swelled. She couldn't imagine life without him. At the passing of his father and mother, he'd assumed his role as king. He'd elected to wear his silver crown for the painting. She'd taken special care to ensure she'd detailed all the fine etchings into the portrait.

The painting was a gift to Noeh, as much from her and Nicholai, as it was from Noeh's grandfather. Family was important, and a sense of happiness enveloped her. To be blessed in love, that was the greatest gift of all.

SOMEWHERE IN THE PACIFIC NORTHWEST
MOUNTAINS - PRESENT DAY

CHAPTER 1

Stale air and mildew assailed Melissa's nose. She tried to swallow, but the thick smell coated her throat. Lifting her head, she opened her eyes. Light blinded her, sending a sharp jolt of pain through her skull. *Where am I?*

She stood erect, her backside pressed against a solid, cold surface. Dampness coated her skin. A thin line of drool spilled from her mouth and onto her chin. She raised her hand to wipe the wetness away, only to discover chains bound her wrists. The iron manacles rattled, echoing off the cement walls. A drop of fear weaseled its way into her mind. She inhaled, and a wave of dizziness passed over her.

The pungent smell of rubbing alcohol filtered into the cell, the telltale sign of Gossum. Melissa's throat constricted, and she gagged. She'd never get used to that stench, not as long as she lived. She winced. That might not be for much longer.

Memories of the Gossum attack raised her pulse and made her shiver. She didn't want to think about why this had happened, why she'd left the safety of her Pride, but she couldn't stop herself. Her heart clenched, and she choked back a sob.

She'd left Denver in search of another Pride, one where maybe, just maybe, she'd be accepted for who she was and not ridiculed for being different. As the only Dren in recent memory to conceive and birth a child, the rest of the Pride either hated her from petty jealousy or wanted to own her. She'd traveled as far as Portland, Oregon, before her need to feed drove her to seek a human male.

Luring a man out of a grocery store late at night, she couldn't bring herself to drink from him. He would've found the sensation pleasurable, and she wouldn't have taken enough blood to kill him, but the human frailty reflected in his eyes, and his likeness to William, her dead mate, had squashed any desire of feeding. She'd fled the scene as far as her feet would take her.

Her enemy found her as she'd stumbled into the warehouse district. Weak from her unwillingness to feed, she wasn't able to maintain her shield. They'd caught her between the old brick buildings. She shuddered at the recollection.

Denver seemed so far away. A ball of regret grew in her stomach. If she'd stayed, she'd be Demir's concubine by now. As ruler of the Pride, he'd wanted her to come to him on her own. When she hadn't, he'd become so enraged she'd feared for her life. What would become of her now? Despair lodged itself in her chest, festering, building until a layer of sweat coated her body.

"Don't fear. They can smell it," a masculine voice said. "They'll be back soon enough."

Across the room, a tall male stood shackled to the wall. Not only did he have arm and leg chains, but cuffs surrounded his neck and torso as well. One arm had a design etched into his skin that ended with four dark lines down the back of his hand. Intelligence shone from one pale blue eye. The other one was darkened with bruising and swollen shut. He looked like he'd seen more than his share of pain and heartache. Although his short brown hair didn't have any grey, the lines in his face indicated he wasn't young. Neither Gossum nor human, he was a species she'd never met.

"Who are you—and where are we?" she asked.

"I'm Gaetan. We're in the Gossum's care, so to speak." His voice was rough, strained.

"Why capture us? Why not just kill us?" The bastard Gossum killed her mate and young son the year before. Her mind fought the horrific images and memories, anything to stop her from going insane with grief. She bit the side of her mouth to stifle a wail of sorrow. Still, a soft whimper escaped.

"That is the question of the hour," he said.

Cuts and bruises marred his arms and legs. When he breathed, his breaths were shallow as if he were in great pain. His left leg was smaller than his right and misshapen, forcing him to lean to the left. They had tortured him. When would they come back to finish the job?

Footsteps approached from the hallway. She tensed, and her pulse pounded in tune with each step.

A Gossum's massive body filled the entrance to her cell. The light from the corridor illuminated him from behind, and his face was a mask of shadows. He snickered. The low sound chilled her arms.

The large male stepped into the chamber, and his features became visible in the dim light. His grim face accentuated his bulbous nose. The brim of his cap covered the back of his neck.

From prior experience with Gossum, she knew he wore the hat to hide his bald head and the beginning of the hard scales that ran down his back. Although once human, he no longer required his eyelids to protect his hard, lizard-like, black eyes. They reflected the light with an eerie shine.

"Ah, good, you're awake. Are you ready to chat?" His menacing voice rasped with venom.

Melissa clamped her lips tight. The steady drip of water nearby echoed against the bare walls. Her damp hair hung in her eyes, the bitterly cold strands clung to her cheeks and arms.

His face turned red at her silence, but he remained calm. He leaned against the wall and crossed his arms. His yellow and black high-tops stood out like a beacon. He could still pass as human, given the right clothing to cover his hairless body and neck scales.

"Ignoring me won't help your cause," he said.

"Don't give in to his demands." Gaetan pulled against his chains.

Their jailer sauntered over to Gaetan. "Still with us, I see." He touched Gaetan's face, raking a claw over his cheek.

Gaetan snarled, and his good eye glowed with specks of gold.

"Oh, yeah, we're making progress." The vile creature chuckled. He turned toward Melissa, and a chilling smile revealed his serrated teeth, the ones he hid from the humans.

She shivered at the sight. Her life couldn't end this way, at the hands of her enemy. Memories of Seth and William raced through her mind, and a knot of determination formed in her stomach. She would fight for them, to honor their memory.

She yanked on her chains but only succeeded in opening cuts on her wrists. Blood trickled over her arm and dripped onto the concrete floor. She wanted to scream her rage at the Gossum, but she held her anger in check, barely.

Like a black cloud, their captor's presence filled the room. Even in his nonchalance his gaze pierced her, held her in place, while a cool bead of sweat rolled down the back of her neck. She feared him, but she wouldn't give her tormentor the satisfaction of seeing her weakness.

"Tell me your name, my dear." His soft and encouraging voice belied his evil intent.

She refused to speak, and instead, raised her chin.

"C'mon now, how is telling me your name going to hurt?" The corner of his mouth pulled into a smile. He returned to Gaetan and pointed, a claw extending like a crooked tree branch from his bony finger near the prisoner's good eye. "I like the sound of his howl. Would you like to hear it?"

Heat flushed through her body. Hatred burned in her gut for what they'd done to Gaetan. She wouldn't be the cause of more pain.

"Melissa," she spat. "My name is Melissa."

"Ah, much better. My name is Ram. Now we are acquainted." Ram placed his index finger next to his mouth and looked at the ceiling. "So, Melissa, about that shield of yours. I could do so much with it."

Melissa flinched at the mention of her gift. She tried to power her energy, but there wasn't even a spark. She held Ram's gaze and struggled to control her shaking knees.

"It's too bad I need you alive to get your blood. Lemurians disintegrate so quickly once dead that I can't get it fast enough." Ram tsked. "So, I'll give you a chance to cooperate."

"I won't give my shield to you." Melissa curled her hands into fists. He wanted her magical power, but no way would she give her special skill to the enemy.

Ram's smile turned into a grimace, and his easygoing demeanor evaporated. He became rigid, his muscles bunching in his arms and legs. His elongated tongue whipped in and out of his mouth, the dangerous spur at the tip coming close to her face.

She recoiled, and her head struck the hard cement wall. Stars swam in her vision, but she refused to succumb to the darkness. Dread snaked its way into her heart.

"As you wish." Ram snapped his fingers.

One of his brood entered the room carrying a cast iron bucket. The top of a branding iron extended over the lip. A towel wrapped around the end protected the handle from the heat within the kettle. The smell of smoldering coal joined with the odors of sweat and fear.

Melissa's pulse quickened. She swallowed, but nothing went down. Her throat was too parched.

Ram grabbed the branding iron.

Adrenaline rushed through her body. "Wh-what is that for?"

"It's your incentive."

"No, don't, not her. Take me." Gaetan's voice, weak and rough, carried across the room.

Melissa glanced at him. They'd just met, but his willingness to protect her spoke volumes about his character.

Ram snapped to attention. "Oh, I intend to get what I need from you, Stiyaha. That abnormal strength of yours will be mine, just not yet. I will take her gift first."

Ram turned his focus back to Melissa. "I want your shield, and I want it now."

He closed the distance, the branding iron's heat radiating in the space between them. Her legs shook, making the shackles at her ankles clank together like an eerie wind chime. Her fear ratcheted up another level, sending a shiver of terror over her shoulders. She hated him all the more.

"Are you willing to bargain? Or are you going to be stubborn?" Ram leaned in, and his breath reeked of liquor. "I know you're Lemurian, but you're not Stiyaha. You must not be from around here. Tell me what you are," he purred, as he drew the back of a finger down the side of her face.

She flinched at his touch, but she wouldn't let him intimidate her. Making eye contact with her enemy, she held her ground.

"If you lead me to others like you, I'll let you walk away, unscathed," he said.

She bared her fangs. "I would never sell out my kind. I will fight you every step of the way."

"Well, now, that's what I thought you'd say." His eyes gleamed with delight, and his mouth curved into a grin. "Let's play, shall we?"

For more information on *Untouchable Lover,* visit www.rosalieredd.com.

ALSO BY ROSALIE REDD

Books in the *Warriors of Lemuria* series:

Untouchable Lover - book #1

Untamable Lover - book #2

Unimaginable Lover - book #3

Undeniable Lover - book #4 - **Coming 2017**

Unforgettable Lover - novella

Alora's Love Potion - short story collection

Marked by Love - novella

Reviews

Enjoyed *Unforgettable Lover*? The best gift you can give an author is an honest review. Please consider leaving a review on your favorite retailer to help spread the word and support an author.

Newsletter

Want access to free reads, special offers, and giveaways? Sign up here for my newsletter on my website and you'll receive a **free ebook**. Don't worry, your information won't be shared with anyone but my muse. You can visit me at my website at www.rosalieredd.com or contact me at Rosalie@rosalieredd.com. I love to receive email from readers!

GLOSSARY

Craya: An expletive.

Gossum: Human converts turned by another Gossum through their bite. They have black eyes, and are hairless, with rough, scalelike skin down their neck and back. Gossum have a spur at the end of their long tongue which they use to paralyze their prey.

Haelen: Healer

Jixies: Small, dwarf-like characters that voluntarily serve the Stiyaha. Jixies tend to be quick, resourceful, and are great planners. Despite their short stature, they can go amongst the humans to obtain special items not made within the Keep.

Keep: The underground home of the Stiyaha and Jixies, located in the mountains of the Pacific Northwest. The Keep is sentient and reacts to her inhabitants with minor tremors and/or by warming or cooling the environment through the sunstones embedded in the walls.

Lemuria: A planet in the Orion constellation. Lemuria is slowly dying and its people must rely on natural resources from other planets to survive.

Lemurians: Refers to both the people on Lemuria, as well as, the characters on Earth. The people of Lemuria appear as gods to the characters in the war on Earth.

Newbs: Young children.

Porte stanen: The massive stone structure in the Portal Navigation Center used to transport characters in and out of the Keep through the portal gateway.

Qithan: Betrothed

Stiyaha: Stoic and just, Stiyaha are noble warriors. Tall and strong, they transform into large beasts, between eight and nine feet tall, covered in fur with large, protruding tusks.

Sunstones: Magical stones that line the ceilings and walls of the Keep, providing heat and light to its inhabitants. Sunstones are used in trade and have some healing abilities.

ABOUT ROSALIE

After finishing a rewarding career in finance and accounting, it was time for award-winning author Rosalie Redd to put away the spread-sheets and take out the word processor. She pens paranormal, science fiction, and fantasy romance in her office cave located in Oregon, where rain is just another excuse to keep writing.